"Are you finally through with this guy now, or what?"

She couldn't help a grin. "Is this on or off the record?"

Frank had the good grace to look embarrassed for asking. "Off."

"We're really through."

"Good." Frank gave her a nod of approval.

"Good?" Cadi felt a tad bewildered by his emphatic reply.

"Well, look. . ." He cleared his throat. "I'll give Marty, the officer in charge, all the information. It's customary for us to do an investigation, particularly since Ross was intoxicated when he got behind the wheel. But I think you should know that I'm requesting to be taken off this case after tonight."

"Why?" She stared into his face, almost losing herself in the depths of his velvety brown eyes. "Am I in trouble?"

He stared back at her. "No, but. . ." He paused. "I think maybe I am."

"Oh?" She hadn't filed any complaints.

She watched in puzzlement as a grin spread across his face.

"I feel like I'm too close to this case, personally, to be objective."

ANDREA BOESHAAR has been married for over thirty years. She and her husband, Daniel, have three marvelous sons, three precious daughters-in-law, and two beautiful grandchildren. Andrea's educational background includes the University of Wisconsin–Milwaukee, where she studied in English, and Alverno College, where she studied Professional Communications and Business Management.

Andrea has been writing stories and poems since she was a little girl; however, it wasn't until 1984 that she started submitting her work for publication. Eight years after that, she was convicted about writing for the Christian market. Since then, she's written numerous articles, novels, and novellas. For more information about Andrea and her books, log onto her Web site at www.andreaboeshaar.com.

HEARTSONG PRESENTS

Don't miss out on any of our super romances. Write to us at the following address for information on our newest releases and club information.

Heartsong Presents Readers' Service
PO Box 721
Uhrichsville, OH 44683

Or visit www.heartsongpresents.com

Courting
Disaster

Andrea Boeshaar

Heartsong Presents

Every book is a team effort, and this novel is no exception. I'd like to express my gratitude to my friend Sally Laity for her critique, and to my copy editor, Deb Peterson, for her time and expertise. I also want to thank my editor, JoAnne Simmons, for giving me the opportunity to write and publish this story. In addition, my deepest thanks to my husband, Daniel, for his love, encouragement, and support. Finally, a very special thank you goes to my nephew Frank Parker for allowing me to use his name and to the good people in Black Hawk County, Iowa, for allowing me to take such liberties with their area. The Village of Wind Lake is fictional, as are its residents.

A note from the Author:
I love to hear from my readers! You may correspond with me by writing:

Andrea Boeshaar
Author Relations
PO Box 721
Uhrichsville, OH 44683

ISBN 978-1-60260-032-4

COURTING DISASTER

All scripture quotations, unless otherwise noted, are taken from the HOLY BIBLE, NEW INTERNATIONAL VERSION®. NIV®. Copyright © 1973, 1978, 1984 by International Bible Society. Used by permission of Zondervan. All rights reserved.

All of the characters and events in this book are fictitious. Any resemblance to actual persons, living or dead, or to actual events is purely coincidental.

Our mission is to publish and distribute inspirational products offering exceptional value and biblical encouragement to the masses.

PRINTED IN THE U.S.A.

one

Cadence Trent forced herself to remain calm even as a searing sense of urgency spread throughout her being. A natural gas explosion. A subdivision almost completely destroyed in Wind Lake. She had to hurry and call the others. Cadi glanced at her wristwatch. Wind Lake was a midsized village on the far northeast side of the county, not too far from where she lived in Waterloo. Still, time was of the essence.

Call Darrell, she reminded herself.

The thought of canceling her date with the handsome honey-blond caused Cadi to cringe. She hated to disappoint him for the umpteenth time. Tonight they planned to go to dinner followed by a concert. Darrell had purchased tickets, and they both had been looking forward to a fun evening out.

Oh, Lord, please help him to understand.

Somehow, in spite of her prayers, Cadi had a hunch he wouldn't.

Weeks ago, Darrell threatened to break off their relationship, stating she put her work before him. He felt Disaster Busters wasn't worth her time and effort. But Cadi knew otherwise. She had experienced the sheer joy of making someone's crisis less devastating. She'd helped victims of tragedy see the rainbow through the rain.

That was one area where she and Darrell disagreed.

Darrell said she had her head in the clouds if she thought Disaster Busters would be a successful venture. He'd given her countless business magazines, encouraging her to "do the math" when it came to Disaster Busters. Cadi knew he meant well, but she also knew her work made her feel needed. She fulfilled a purpose, and God provided and blessed the rest. So she forged onward. She never meant to take Darrell for granted, but like today, duty called and she had to go; there were people without homes, food, and clothing because of a natural gas explosion in their community. Her nonprofit organization, Disaster Busters, had been summoned to provide these victims with basic needs. How could she refuse?

Very simply, she couldn't.

The wooden steps of the old Victorian home creaked as Cadi took them two at a time. Upstairs, she hurried down the narrow hallway and into the bedroom. She grabbed the overnight bag she always kept packed with extra clothes and personal accessories and just about everything else. She picked up her purse, slinging its leather strap over her shoulder, and ran back down to the first floor.

"What's all the commotion?" Aunt Lou entered the foyer from the kitchen, wiping her nimble hands on the colorful apron drawn about her thick waist. As always, her dusky gray hair was swirled elaborately around her head and at the sides of her face in a creation she called "Queen Elizabeth" fashion. Cadi had to agree the style made the older woman appear both regal and ageless.

"Sounds like cannonballs bouncing down the steps."

Cadi couldn't help the smirk tugging at the corners of her mouth. "You can recall what cannonballs sound like?"

"I was hardly referring to my age." Aunt Lou clucked her tongue. "Sassy girl."

She laughed. "Sorry about the noise. Another call came in."

"Oh. . ." A frown wrinkled her gray brows. "How long will you be gone?"

"Not sure. Just depends." Noticing her aunt's concerned expression, she added, "An explosion in Wind Lake. The building is a complete loss."

"How awful. Anyone hurt?"

"Several injuries, but no one was killed as far as I know. Emergency personnel are still on the scene."

"How dreadful." Aunt Lou's frown of concern gave way to an encouraging grin. "Well, I'll call Lonnie Mae and the other members of our prayer chain. We'll cover you."

"Thanks. I don't know what I'd do without you." Cadi kissed her aunt's cheek then dashed outside to her minivan. A gentle May breeze tousled her short hair and wafted through the budding treetops.

Opening the van door, she tossed her purse and overnight bag into the vehicle before climbing behind the wheel. She started the engine then slowly backed out of the driveway and into the street. She took one last look toward the house. Her aunt stood on the porch and waved. Cadi returned the gesture then put the transmission into drive and stepped on the accelerator.

Cadi felt a grin pull at the corners of her lips. Aunt Lou, bless her heart. The very thought of the woman caused a swell of gratitude to plume within her. Her aunt was the most giving and caring person in Cadi's life. What's more, Aunt Lou had been her parental figure since Cadi was eleven years old. Aunt Lou, in her seventies now and her great-aunt, actually, had taken Cadi in after her parents and younger brother and sister drowned when the Mississippi overflowed its banks. Cadi could still recall the tragedy vividly.

It had rained for days, but it seemed like a regular Sunday evening to Cadi when she and her family ventured off to the evening service at church. Minutes later their car stalled in a flooded intersection. The water kept rising and rising until Dad instructed all of them to climb up onto the roof of the sedan. Darkness fell hard and fast, making their predicament all the more harrowing. There were others stranded, too, and the cries for help, the screams of fear, barely rose above the din of the rushing floodwater. Within a short period of time, Cadi and her family were swept off the car. Cadi had gulped for air and fought against the unmerciful current for what seemed like hours. Then, miraculously, a rescue worker plucked her from the surge.

The bodies of her parents and siblings were found a few days later.

Oh, Lord. . . Cadi closed her eyes, trying to quell the painful memory.

The driver in the car behind her honked, and she gave herself a mental shake. The past was just that: the past. No sense in reliving it, although Cadi's past was why she'd gone to school and become an emergency medical technician. Next she began the Disaster Busters organization. She wanted to help other victims of tragedies—like those in today's explosion.

The urgency of the situation caught up with her, and Cadi realized she hadn't called her colleagues, Bailey, Jeff, Megan, and Will. They had full-time jobs of their own but were still vital volunteers that kept Disaster Busters functional. Cadi tried to pay them with love offerings and donations that Disaster Busters received. Many times, paying them resulted in Cadi forfeiting her salary and, just as she had in the past, Aunt Lou came to the rescue. It was a sacrifice on her aunt's part, too.

Steering her van to the side of the road, Cadi fished her cell phone from her purse. Within minutes, she had placed the calls. All four assistants said they were available and could help, and Cadi arranged to meet them at the Disaster Busters office located inside Riverview Bible Church.

Next, it was time to call Darrell. She pressed in his number on the keypad of her phone and plugged in her hands-free device. She pulled away from the curb, sending up another silent prayer that he'd understand.

Darrell answered on the third ring. His reaction was just as Cadi feared.

"What? You're canceling on me again?"

She grimaced. "Sorry."

"We've got dinner reservations. I bought tickets for the concert afterward!"

Cadi imagined the angry sparks flashing in Darrell's hazel eyes. "Look, I apologize for backing out on our date, but the team and I—"

"The team. Right." Darrell paused. "Those friends of yours

aren't going to help you make important contacts. Success means rubbing elbows with the right people. But I guess you proved to me once again that *the team* will always come before anything we might have together."

Cadi opened her mouth to refute his statements, but she couldn't. Aunt Lou's not-so-subtle remarks filled her mind. *"He's not a patient man, is he? Patience is a virtue, you know."*

Had Aunt Lou seen something amiss in Cadi's relationship with Darrell Barclay from the beginning?

"Cadi? Are you there?"

Darrell's deep voice rattled her. "I'm here." She squared her shoulders, remembering her mission at hand. She couldn't afford to let her emotions get in the way right now. She had a job to do, and she had to be strong—strong in the Lord. "Darrell, let's talk about this later, okay?"

"No need. As long as your loser business comes before me, I have nothing more to say."

She clenched her jaw. "Loser business?"

"That's what I said."

"I explained all this to you before."

"And I don't want to hear it again."

"Fine. If that's how you feel—"

"That's exactly how I feel. There are plenty of girls waiting in line to take your place in my life."

Shock enveloped Cadi. Had she heard correctly? Seconds later, she realized her hearing was just fine, and oddly enough the barb didn't sting as much as she thought it might.

"You know, if I'm that replaceable, Darrell, then you shouldn't be so irate that I'm canceling our date tonight."

"Yeah, whatever."

"I have to go." She paused. "Good-bye, Darrell."

She didn't wait for a reply. Ending the call, she removed her earpiece and set it and the phone on the console between the van's two front seats. She suspected it was the end of her short-lived romance with Darrell, and while she didn't feel heartbroken, exactly, she had to admit to a deep sense of disappointment. Someday she'd like to get married and have a family—a large family.

She quieted her straying thoughts and tightened her grip on the steering wheel. No time to fantasize about the future. There was a crisis at hand.

She forced her attention back to the present and turned her car into Riverview's vast parking lot. Almost a year ago, Cadi's pastor and the deacons agreed to lease her office space for Disaster Busters, and they encouraged her to fulfill her mission to help people in need. Remembering her pastor's kind words now seemed like a salve of comfort after Darrell's mean remark. "Loser business."

What does he know?

Cadi stepped down from her vehicle and shoved Darrell from her mind. She began forming a mental list of the supplies that she and her team needed to pack: blankets, clothing, nonperishable food items. . .

She crossed the parking lot and entered the side door of the large church. The soles of her white athletic shoes squeaked on the polished tile floor in the empty hallway. She reached the Disaster Busters office, and when she opened the door, the sight that greeted her erased any defeat she might have felt after her conversation with Darrell. There, packing boxes of foodstuff, were two members of her team.

"Bailey's gathering up some blankets," Jeff said as he lifted a box and handed it to Will.

"And I'll take this out to the trailer." Will motioned to the box with his head. "While I'm out there, I'll hitch it to the van."

"I'll come out and help," Jeff said.

"You guys are awesome." Cadi glanced from one to the other.

Then Will jutted out his narrow hip, and she tucked her car keys into the back pocket of his blue jeans.

Moments later she, too, set to task. She placed various items in crates and boxes. All the while she marveled at how close she and her team had grown since the inception of Disaster Busters just shy of a year ago. She had been a bridesmaid in Jeff and Bailey's wedding and attended Bailey's graduation from nursing school. Will acted like Cadi's big brother. They'd known each other since they were foster kids who'd wound up in the same home for almost two years before the state located Aunt Lou. Nevertheless, the joke remained that she and Will were siblings, although jest became reality in a spiritual way when Will asked Jesus Christ into his heart as a teenager. So when Cadi introduced him to Darrell, Will had light-heartedly said, "You be good to my baby sister, now, or I'll come lookin' for you."

Darrell had appeared confused as he peered from Cadi's Scandinavian, peaches-and-cream complexion to Will, whose African-American heritage shone proudly from his dark brown eyes. "You're brother and sister?"

"Same heavenly Father." Will sported a broad grin.

"Oh. Right." Darrell had quickly changed the subject. Obviously he wasn't amused.

"No patience, no imagination, and no sense of humor," Cadi muttered as she folded and packed some clothing items from the clothes pantry in back of the office. The room was no bigger than a large closet.

"What did you say?"

Cadi whirled around and saw her best friend, Megan Buckingham, standing there with arms akimbo. Cadi shook her head. "Nothing. I mean, I didn't say anything worth repeating."

"Hmm, well let me take a guess." Megan tipped her head. Strands of her walnut brown hair fell across her preseason tanned cheek, evidence of the tanning booth she liked to frequent. "You canceled your date with Darrell, and he was anything but understanding."

"Bingo."

Meg flicked her gaze toward the dimpled ceiling. "Typical." She blew out a puff of air. "Well, he'll get over it."

Cadi shook her head. "Not this time, he won't. I think Darrell and I are through unless I beg and plead, which I won't. Not again."

Megan paused for several seconds. "Maybe it's for the best."

"I'm sure it's for the best. . .at least now I'm sure."

"About time," Megan quipped. "I thought you'd never come to your senses. I've said it all along: Darrell is a fake. I've been praying you'd see through his facade."

"Maybe you're right. It's just that I want a family of my own someday, and—"

"And Darrell's an eligible bachelor," Meg cut in. "He's good-looking, and he has a nice career going for him. But those aren't enough reasons to actually *marry* the guy."

"Meg, I see the positive in everyone. I can look beyond the. . .*the facade.*"

"Well, in Darrell's case, there's not much more to see, okay?" A teasing grin spread across Meg's face.

Cadi had to smile. "Seems I had to find that out the hard way."

Compassion filled Meg's iridescent brown eyes. "Oh, you're really hurt, aren't you?" She wrapped her long, slender arms around Cadi. "I'm so sorry."

She returned the hug. "I'm okay."

At that moment, Will strode back in from the parking lot. "I'm ready to take the next box to the trailer, and then I think we're all packed up and ready to go."

❧

Black Hawk County sheriff's deputy Patrol Sergeant Frank Parker slowed traffic on the highway leading into town and directed motor vehicles and curious bystanders away from the emergency personnel. Wind Lake didn't get a whole lot of traffic, but most of its population, along with tourists arriving for the Memorial Day weekend, had come out to glimpse the devastation that the natural gas explosion caused. Homes in the newly constructed subdivision still smoldered, and debris littered the area.

"Stay off the street, folks," he said to the collecting crowd. "Move back."

A few people paused to ask questions, and some waved a greeting and called him by name. Frank took a special interest in this assignment. Born and raised here, he made his home in Wind Lake. In short, this village wasn't just the place in which he lived; it was his jurisdiction, along with the two adjacent townships. Placing sheriff deputies in their hometowns was all part of the county's Know Your Neighbors program.

Out of the corner of his eye, Frank saw movement and turned in time to see Erin Potter's red hair as she ducked around him. She worked for the *Village Gazette*. Frank watched her lift her high-speed camera then heard its shutter clicking as she snapped several photos. He gave her a good thirty seconds before calling her back behind the yellow plastic tape.

"You're a peach, Frank," she said with a wink. "I can always count on you to let me behind the barrier for a couple moments so I can get my pictures."

"Don't let that get around, Erin."

The slender, middle-aged woman chuckled and trotted back to the sidewalk, her ponytail swinging from side to side.

It wasn't but a minute later when a light blue minivan made its way down the street. Frank began shaking his head in a nonverbal warning so the vehicle wouldn't proceed further. The van continued on a few feet then rolled to a stop. Frank cautiously approached. The window slid down, and a young woman leaned her head out. His first thought was that she had the hugest sky blue eyes he'd ever seen.

"Disaster Busters reporting for duty."

And a sunny smile.

"They're expecting us."

Frank drew his chin back. "I beg your pardon?"

"We're the Disaster Busters team."

"Never heard of you." Frank noticed how the woman's layered blond hair flipped upward at the ends.

"We're a nonprofit organization out of Waterloo. We're here to help the victims of the explosion."

"We're a charity group!" the brunette in the passenger seat called to him.

The words "nonprofit organization" and "charity group" set off warning bells inside his head. "Got any ID?"

"Absolutely." The blond driver handed him her Iowa driver's license and a business card.

"Cadence Trent. Disaster Busters, eh?" He eyed the young woman and her passengers with skepticism. He knew firsthand the scams and schemes associated with tragedies. Victims were vulnerable, and part of his job was to protect them. "Sorry. I wasn't told you have security clearance, so turn the vehicle around."

"But—"

"You heard me. Turn around." He extended his hand to return the driver's ID.

"Officer!" A male voice hailed him. "Wait a minute, Officer!"

Frank wheeled around in time to see Harrison Elliot, Wind Lake's mayor, striding toward him.

"Is this the team from Waterloo? Five people in all? We've been expecting them." He sidled up to the minivan. "You must be Cadi."

"Yes. And you must be Mayor Elliot."

"I am he." There was a smile in his voice, but when he turned to Frank, he scowled. "Let this van pass, Officer."

"If you say so."

"I do, indeed."

Frank tensed in protest then returned the ID and took a step back. He observed the blond tuck the identification into a long, trim billfold before she gave him a smile. A semblance of a peace offering, perhaps, but Frank wasn't won over that easily.

"Pull forward, Cadi," Mayor Elliot said. "Park over there. Pastor Dremond is setting up some tables, and we're inviting those who are homeless because of this terrible tragedy to register."

At the mention of Adam Dremond's name, Frank's tension abated somewhat. He knew Adam personally, and he was a good man. The mayor, on the other hand, was more pomp than circumstance as far as Frank was concerned.

Meanwhile, Cadi drove forward.

"I summoned the Disaster Busters team," the stocky mayor informed Frank with a set to his jaw. "You had no business trying to turn them away."

"In all due respect, sir, if you had informed the Sheriff's Department of their expected arrival—"

"I did," he groused.

"Nothing came over the radio."

Elliot waved one beefy hand in the air. "Ooooh, I don't have time to argue the point. Just—just go about your business."

To his credit, Frank didn't even grin at the sputtered remark. Nevertheless, he bristled at the mayor's less-than-perfect handling of the situation. As for that little Disaster Buster, she might have clearance from Elliot, but that didn't mean her organization was really on the up-and-up.

Frank decided he'd better keep his eye on her.

two

"She's all right, Frank."

"How do you know?" He watched Cadi and her crew from out of the corner of his eye. They stood behind a long, rectangular table set up under a blue, twelve-by-twelve tarp. The Disaster Busters registered the recently homeless and orchestrated temporary arrangements, courtesy of a local establishment called the Wind Lake Inn and several charitable residents. "What if they're rip-off artists?"

"I meet a group of local pastors for lunch every few months, and John Connor, Cadi Trent's pastor, is one of them." Adam grinned and finger-combed his thick, reddish brown hair off his forehead. "She comes highly recommended."

Frank turned toward him. He and Adam Dremond had known each other for years, ever since the reverend arrived in Wind Lake. Adam was something of a social activist, but he operated aboveboard and made it a point to get to know law enforcement officials. His cooperation paid off. The entire sheriff's department had come to respect Adam.

"So give me the lowdown on these Disaster Busters." Ordinarily Frank trusted his friend's word, but he still had his qualms about this group of strangers.

"Well, from what I understand, it's a faith-based organization, but it works with local government. I convinced the mayor to give Cadi's group a chance, and since there was a lot of bureaucratic red tape to cut through in order for county, state, or federal assistance to get here, Mayor Elliot was all for it."

"Hmm. . ." Frank tucked his thumbs into the thick belt strapped around his waist. He watched as Cadi's slender form bent and she wrote something on the paper in front of her. He had to admit she made a fetching sight, even in an ordinary pink polo shirt and faded blue jeans. Then, when she came around the table and placed her arm around the shoulders of a disheveled elderly woman, an odd sense of longing gripped him.

He shook it off and pulled his gaze away from Cadi. "She looks young."

"Midtwenties is my guess."

"I suppose that makes her old enough to be capable of an undertaking such as this," he muttered, even though at thirty-four he wasn't all that much older than she; however, he felt as if he'd lived an entire life—and that life ended some three years ago. Now his days were but twenty-four-hour capsules of existence—except around his two children. If it weren't for them, he wouldn't feel alive at all. He wouldn't feel—period.

"I'm told Cadi is more than capable. So are her associates. Cadi is an experienced EMT, and there's a registered nurse in the group, along with a guy who's a family counselor."

"Sounds like they're qualified." After several pensive moments, he regarded Adam again and decided to voice his concerns. "Remember the tornado that hit a few years back?"

The pastor's usually jovial expression was replaced by a look of remorse. "Of course I remember. Who could forget it?"

Frank knew that *he* would never forget it. The storm had snuffed out the bright and beautiful life of his beloved wife and left him with two small children to raise. He was only too grateful for his extended family members who, between them, provided day care so Frank could keep his job. "There was a charity group that came in to help after the twister hit." He glanced back at the Disaster Busters group. "They seemed just as qualified and capable, but those guys looted our ravaged community and swindled the most vulnerable. To this day, there are those who haven't recovered."

"I'm well aware of that unfortunate incident, but Cadi's company isn't like that, okay?" Empathy shone from Adam's hazel eyes. "And maybe it's time you started trusting people again."

Frank guarded his reaction. "Maybe." He watched as Cadi conversed with two teenagers.

"We'd also love to see you in church again."

He swung his gaze back to Adam and noticed the twinkle in his eyes. "You've always got to work church into a conversation, don't you?"

Adam nodded. "It's my job."

"Yeah, I know." Frank couldn't help but grin, but just as soon as it appeared, he felt it slip from his lips. "Look, my relationship with the Lord is intact."

"Don't you want more than that? Don't you desire a closer walk with God and fellowship with other like-minded believers?"

"Sure, but attending church isn't easy."

Frank stopped short of admitting that on Sunday mornings when he thought of attending worship services, sudden memories of his wife, Yolanda, dashed his concerted efforts and left him feeling depressed and hopeless. In his mind's eye, he could see her preparing breakfast. He could practically hear her humming while she dressed the kids in their Sunday best. It was all Frank could do to keep from breaking down in front of his children. As if that wasn't bad enough, when he did manage to attend services, he was bombarded with sad, piteous stares from everyone who knew Yolanda. It was more than he could bear. So, typically, he waited until his mother-in-law picked up Dustin and Emily for Sunday school before he went to work early. Then he pushed his feelings into the farthest corner of his heart.

He cleared the discomfort from his throat. "I'm sure I'll get to church again eventually."

"If not ours then perhaps another solid, Bible-believing church."

"Yeah." Frank was amazed at how the man had divined his thoughts. "Maybe."

"Hearing God's Word will strengthen your faith. Fellowship with other believers will encourage you."

Frank smirked. "I get the message already."

Adam smiled and gave him a friendly slap between the shoulder blades. "All right. I've needled you enough for one day. Besides, I've got other work to do." He inclined his head toward the many explosion victims. "See ya later."

"Yeah. . .see you."

৯

"What's with that sheriff's deputy?"

Cadi followed her friend's line of vision and glimpsed the tall, broad-shouldered man with short, jet black hair. He seemed to scowl at her and Meg.

"And why is he staring at us like we're convicted bank robbers? We're here to help."

"Maybe he's having a bad day," Cadi said. "Try to ignore him." Her suggestion belied the nervous anticipation winding its way around her insides—like the feeling that threatened whenever she spoke in front of large audiences. Now, as she did then, Cadi silently recited her favorite passage of scripture, Philippians 4:6–7. *"Do not be anxious about anything, but in everything, by prayer and petition, with thanksgiving, present your requests to God. And the peace of God, which transcends all understanding, will guard your hearts and your minds in Christ Jesus."*

"Um, I don't think we're going to be able to ignore that guy, Cadi." The warning in her friend's voice rang out loud and clear. "He's heading our way."

She glanced up from her yellow legal pad and met the gaze of the stern-faced deputy.

"Ladies," he said with a slight dip of his head when he reached them. "Anything I can do to assist you?"

Was he serious? Cadi sensed a measure of condescension in his tone. "We're okay, but thanks anyway."

The deputy shifted his stance. "I think maybe we got off to a bad start." He extended his right hand. "I'm Sergeant Frank Parker."

"Cadi Trent." She set her palm inside his much larger one.

He gave it a firm but cordial shake that stayed with her long after he released her hand. Cadi turned toward her friend. "This is Meg Buckingham."

"Good to meet you both." Frank cleared his throat before glancing over his shoulder. He looked a mite uneasy, and it gave Cadi a small measure of comfort to think she wasn't the only one.

"Well, I'd best get back to work, unless there's anything you ladies need."

"There is one thing," Meg said before turning to Cadi. "Tell him about the two teenagers."

"Will and Pastor Dremond are taking care of them."

"Perhaps I can help."

Cadi regarded the man, noticing his large build and scrutinizing deep brown eyes. Along with his shadowed jaw, Cadi thought he made an imposing figure.

"Miss Trent? Or is it Mrs. Trent?"

"Miss." She felt almost mesmerized.

"Extremely *Miss* after today," Meg piped up, putting Cadi on sudden alert. "She and her boyfriend called it quits this afternoon."

"Meg!" She rapped her friend's upper arm. "I'm sure the officer here isn't interested in my personal issues." She felt her cheeks growing hot with embarrassment.

"Sorry to hear about the breakup, *Miss* Trent."

Awkwardness seemed to envelop her, but at least the man appeared sincere.

"Thanks." She managed a shrug and muttered, "It's for the best."

"Definitely for the best," Meg reiterated with a pointed look at Cadi. "Now about those kids; we're trying to locate their parents."

"What's the last name?" Frank pulled a small notebook from his back pocket and flipped it open.

Cadi looked at her pad of paper. "Jenkins. Their mom's first name is Loretta, and their dad's is Brett."

"Loretta and Brett Jenkins?" Frank wrote down the names, while shaking his head. "Don't believe I know either of them. They're obviously not locals. But I'll radio it in. We'll find 'em." With a nod and a small smile, he turned on his heel and took purposeful strides toward the white squad car with the words BLACK HAWK COUNTY SHERIFF painted across the doors in bold yellow letters.

"Maybe he's not such a crabby guy after all," Meg remarked, watching him go.

"Yeah, but you've got a big mouth." Cadi expelled a breath laden with aggravation. "How could you bring up my relationship with Darrell to a complete stranger?"

Meg faced her and seemed at a loss for words. "I—I don't know. I didn't mean to. It just tumbled out of my mouth. Once I'd blurted the news, I tried to make the best of it." She stepped forward and grabbed hold of Cadi's wrist. "I'm sorry. Will you forgive me? You know I don't make a habit of spouting off my best friend's personal information—or anyone else's for that matter. I'm usually very discreet."

Cadi couldn't argue. "Oh, let's just forget it, okay? Of course I forgive you!"

Meg beamed and gave her a quick hug. "I'll go tell Will and Pastor Dremond that we've got the sheriff's department helping us find the Jenkinses."

Cadi replied with a nod and resumed her post at the table. Bailey and Jeff were talking to another young couple. She listened in for a few minutes, and her heart broke to hear how the newlyweds lost almost everything in the explosion that damaged their home.

That's why I'm here, Lord, she thought. *I'm here to represent You with love and compassion and help lighten these people's loads.*

Her gaze roamed beyond the two couples and to the dark-haired sheriff's deputy standing next to his vehicle, its driver's side door wide open. He had placed his foot on the doorjamb while he penned something into his notebook, using his knee for a writing surface.

In the next second he looked up, and his dark eyes riveted her so that all she could do was stare back at him.

"Hey, Cadi, I'm looking for that box of men's clothes—Cadi? Yo, Cadi."

She felt a hand on her shoulder and the mild shake that followed.

"What?" She turned to find Will standing beside her. She collected her wits. "What are you looking for?"

"The deputy, huh?" A playful grin spread across Will's face. "Are you one of those women who can't resist a man in uniform?" He chuckled.

"Oh, hush." Cadi brushed his hand off her shoulder.

Will laughed again. "You're a free agent now, you know? Darrell is his-tor-eee."

She felt the deep frown creasing her brow. "Stop teasing me."

He shaded his amusement with feigned professionalism. "Have you seen the box of men's clothing? I'm working with several individuals who could use a few pairs of pants and several shirts."

Cadi pulled the minivan's keys from her jeans pocket and set them none-too-gently into Will's awaiting palm.

He gave her a gracious bow before walking away.

What a clown, Cadi thought in his wake. But what would she ever do without Will around to make her smile? He was like sunshine in the midst of the storm.

Or, in this case, *explosion.*

Cadi's musing came back around to the present tragedy, which, in turn, made her think about the nice-looking sheriff's deputy with the austere demeanor.

But when she looked his way again, she noticed that a different officer stood at the barricade, deterring onlookers. The squad car was gone, and Frank Parker was nowhere in sight.

three

Frank squelched his impatience as Julie, an administrative assistant, ran a search on Cadi. Almost a half hour later, the plump brunette returned to the cubicle that surrounded his cluttered desk and shared what she'd found.

"The search came up empty."

"Good." Seeing Julie's curious expression, he immediately recanted his all-too-eager reply. "Um—it's good news for the community."

Her look of interest waned.

"I wouldn't want folks in Wind Lake to get swindled by con artists," he added. "It would be the nightmare of three years ago revisited."

"Oh, right. I remember that. My cousin and his wife were out their entire home insurance check because those supposed do-gooders helped them with the forms and conveniently had the check sent to them. They stole it."

"Exactly what I don't ever want to happen again." Frank, too, had lost more than his beloved wife. Stating they would "clean up" his damaged property, the phony charity group looted everything of value.

With a bob of her head, Julie headed for her own work area near the front of the sheriff department's satellite office.

Frank lazed back in his worn leather swivel chair. Out of habit he lifted a pen from the desk and tapped it against the metal finish while he pondered the situation. He had to admit to feeling relieved that Miss Cadi Trent had no criminal history. But why should he care if she did? And why couldn't he rid his memory of her arresting blue eyes? So what if she'd just broken up with her boyfriend? None of his concern.

Frank shook his head, disrupting his wayward thought

process. What mattered to him was enforcing the law and protecting the citizens of Black Hawk County. Nothing more. Nothing less.

He stood and tossed the pen aside. He had work to do. No time for half-baked musings. Mayor Elliot had decided to hold a community barbecue in one of the county's many parks. This particular one, Lakeview Park, had a large, covered picnic area. The outing had been a spur-of-the-moment idea, and Frank supposed it was a good way of feeding those left homeless today and thanking all the volunteers who'd teamed together to help emergency personnel after this afternoon's explosion. Frank would be there; the park was part of his jurisdiction.

He collected his gear and strode outside to the patrol car. Expectancy pervaded his being. Would Cadi be at the barbecue?

It's none of my business unless she's doing something illegal.

He tried in vain to squelch further thoughts of the curvy blond with the enormous eyes. Okay, so he found her attractive. He'd admit at least that much. Except his emotions wanted to take a step further, and that was far from typical for him. He thought he'd become immune to feminine charm. What was going on?

It's the long hours I've been working. . . .

Seconds later, a very different idea struck. Maybe this was part of her plan. Distract the sheriff's department. Befriend the mayor. Disarm them all with her wiles and then—*bam!* Cadi and her Disaster Busters could scam poor, unsuspecting souls in no time.

A tight grin pulled at his mouth as he started the vehicle's engine. Now things made more sense.

❧

"It's five dollars for adults and two dollars for kids under twelve," Cadi informed the gathering crowd pressing in on her. She pointed at the sign she'd made earlier. "All the money raised will be divided and distributed to the victims of today's disaster."

A queue had already formed, and Will, Bailey, and Jeff collected the money. After people paid, they filed in under the large roofed picnic area and claimed tables for themselves and family members. Meanwhile, the grills, attended by volunteers, smoked outside the open-ended shelter.

Mayor Elliot told Cadi the village would take care of the cost of the hamburgers and hot dogs, while a local grocery store donated buns and condiments along with carrots, pickles, and potato salad. Cadi had never been so impressed with a community coming together to help each other. Even now several female residents of Wind Lake were arranging the food table in preparation for the huge buffet, and folks were beginning to help themselves to the fare.

"This was a great idea, Cadi." The mayor stood beside her and watched the goings-on. He puffed out his chest beneath the dark blue cotton dress shirt he wore tucked into his tan trousers. "I'm glad I thought of it."

"So am I. We've got a great turnout."

He nodded then snapped his pudgy fingers. "I almost forgot—I've made arrangements for you and your friends to stay at the Wind Lake Inn tonight."

"Thank you, but it's not necessary. We can drive back to Waterloo."

"No, no. I insist. It'll be dark and very late by the time our fund-raiser ends tonight. I'm sure you and your crew will be exhausted, and the hotel is very comfortable."

"Well, then, all right." Cadi saw the wisdom in the mayor's decision. "Thank you. We appreciate it."

A glitter in the distance caught her eye and she turned in time to see Sergeant Frank Parker making purposeful strides toward them. His shiny badge reflected the late afternoon sun. To Cadi, the deputy looked as daunting as an approaching thunderstorm.

The mayor must have noticed her sudden discomfort. "Some people take themselves far too seriously," he said with a glance in Frank's direction. "Don't let him cow you."

She laughed to cover her unease. "Don't worry. I won't."

"Good." Mayor Elliot gave her shoulder a pat of encouragement and sauntered off to greet several members of the media. He seemed in his element as he spoke to reporters.

Cadi grinned and moved to find something to do to help with the barbecue, but before she could inch forward, Frank Parker stepped into her path.

She sucked in a startled breath. When she last saw him, he'd been nearer to the street than the tent.

"Hello, Sergeant." She gathered her wits again, which she seemed to be having trouble keeping track of around this man. He seemed like a towering oak tree at this close proximity.

"Looks like a lot of money you're collecting there." He flicked a glance in Will, Bailey, and Jeff's direction. "I thought tonight was supposed to be a free event to thank the volunteers and emergency personnel."

She caught his meaning. "Oh, well, if it's the five dollars you're worried about, forget it. You can eat for free. After all, you helped this afternoon, too."

She stepped to the side and once more Frank blocked her way.

"That's not what I'm getting at."

"Oh?" Cadi felt confused.

"The money you're collecting. . ." A dark frown deepened his shadowed features. "I suppose it's for charitable purposes. Or is it to pay your expenses?"

"What?" She tipped her head then gave it a shake. "Listen, if it's a permit you're looking for, ask the mayor."

"The money, *Miss* Trent. Where's it going?"

The slur was unmistakable, and while Cadi could usually handle herself in a dignified manner, she felt close to losing her patience with this man. "If it's all right with you," she began facetiously, "we plan to divide up the money at the end of the night and give it to the victims of today's explosion."

"Oh, yeah?" He leaned forward, and Cadi got a whiff of some tangy scent he wore. "Well, I'm going to personally see to it that the victims get that money. Every last penny."

At first Cadi didn't understand, but then it dawned on her like a brilliant sunrise.

"Are you implying I'm some sort of thief?" She placed her hands on her hips and raised her chin.

"Maybe you are and maybe you aren't." He stood to his full height, which Cadi guessed to be well over six feet. "All I know for sure is that I'm here to protect the citizens of Wind Lake."

"Kind of like a vicious watchdog, eh?" Indignation sliced through her. "Well, I'll be sure to *whistle* for you when we're ready to count the money—unless you'd like to stand guard over it all night. We have nothing to hide, so whatever you decide is fine with me and my team."

He stood statue still as though stunned by her reply and Cadi thought she saw a sparkle of amusement in his brown eyes—unless it was raw infuriation.

No. It was amusement. Definitely amusement.

Cadi felt her tense muscles relax somewhat, but in the next moment her attention was captured by the little girl dressed in a yellow, hooded sweatshirt and brightly printed corduroy slacks who'd flung herself around Deputy Parker's tree trunk of a leg.

"Daddy!" she squealed.

"Hi, Emmie." A smile lit his face like a flame in the darkness. He lifted the girl into his arms. Moments later a boy about eight or nine years old appeared. His greeting, like his attire, was much more subdued, and Cadi watched as he leaned against Frank's hip. "Hello, son." He tousled the boy's hair with his free hand.

Cadi watched in sheer amazement as the stony officer, who'd given her a difficult time since her arrival, morphed into some warm and fuzzy creature right before her very eyes.

She folded her arms. "I get the feeling that your bark is worse than your bite, Sergeant Parker." She grinned, feeling disarmed.

"These are my kids," Frank began proudly, despite the choke hold his daughter had him in. "Emily and Dustin."

"Nice to meet you both." She thought his children were beautiful with their golden-brown hair and amber eyes. "I'm Cadi." She glanced around, expecting to see a Mrs. Parker nearby. When the moments that ticked by didn't produce his wife, Cadi's curiosity mounted. The kids couldn't have appeared out of nowhere.

What do I care if he's married or not?

"Well, I need to get back to work," she said.

"Sure. Just *whistle* if you need anything."

The sarcastic quip wasn't lost on her. She grinned and busied herself with the numerous tasks at hand.

❧

After his mother fed the kids and took them home, Frank devoted his time to the steadfast scrutiny of the Disaster Busters team, particularly its leader, Cadi Trent. He had to admit he liked the way her short blond hair flipped up all over, matching her sassy personality. When he first confronted her about the donation money, he thought he'd scared her, and his conscience pricked. But soon he realized they could match wits with little effort.

Vicious watchdog. Yeah, right!

Frank stifled the oncoming snicker and watched Cadi interact with the community. Most of the older citizens in Wind Lake knew each other, although the village had expanded. Cabins now lined the nearby lake, and novelty shops sprouted along Main Street. Soon tourists would be tying up intersections and crowding sidewalks. There would be boating accidents and petty thefts to investigate, not to mention the bar fights to break up in the wee hours of the morning. The handful of police the village employed during tourist season couldn't keep up with the problems, and Frank knew from years gone by that the sheriff's department would be busy.

"Frank! Oh, Frank Parker!"

He turned and found Mrs. Corbin at his side. She'd been a schoolteacher in her younger days, and Frank knew her from church—when he used to attend regularly, that is.

The elderly woman placed her hand on his arm. "See that girl in the pink shirt?"

He followed her gaze to Cadi. "Yes, ma'am. I see her." He'd been watching her all night.

"Well, she's the nicest thing. She's agreed to help my friend Bettyanne file an insurance claim." A nippy gust of wind blew strands of her short white hair off her wrinkled forehead. "Bettyanne lost almost all of her belongings this afternoon. Such a shame. She'd just moved into that new duplex. She was renting, you know? Everything was so clean and nice. . . ."

Frank's ears had perked up at the mention of filing an insurance claim.

"And her antiques. . . Bettyanne loved to hit the antique shops on Thursday afternoons. Of course, the ones around here in town are far too commercial for her liking. Bettyanne prefers estate sales where she can find the true deals."

"Cadi offered to file an insurance claim for her?"

"Yes, that's right." The woman straightened her spindly frame. She stood all of five feet. "Cadi said she's staying overnight and she'd call the insurance company for Bettyanne tomorrow morning. They're meeting at the bank around nine o'clock. Bettyanne has her policy in a safe deposit box. Good thing that didn't go up in flames."

"Yes, ma'am." Suspicion reared its ugly head, and Frank clenched his jaw.

"Isn't that good of Cadi?" Mrs. Corbin prattled on. "She's a nice girl. Cadi asked Bettyanne if she needed housing, but she's going to move in with me for the time being."

"Nice girl, yeah." Frank's gaze burned into Cadi's shapely form. So the scamming had begun. He looked back down at Mrs. Corbin. "Thanks for letting me know."

"Oh, of course. Bettyanne's so relieved that she remembered she purchased a renter's insurance policy. I'm glad, too, that she might be the least bit compensated for her loss." Mrs. Corbin smiled. "But that's what insurance is for, isn't it?"

"That's right." He pushed out a smile for her benefit then meandered over to where Cadi stood over a box of clothing. She rummaged through its contents.

"I hear you've agreed to help an elderly lady file an insurance claim."

"What?" Cadi brought up her head so fast that she almost caught Frank right in the chin.

"Insurance claims—do you have experience filing them?"

She straightened. "Not really, but I can probably stumble through the process."

She tipped her head, and even in the dim lighting of the battery-operated lanterns, Frank could still see the curiosity that shimmered in her blue eyes. Then she shivered and looked back into the cardboard box.

"I know there's a clean sweatshirt in here. . . ."

In spite of himself, Frank assisted her in locating the thick, zippered garment before helping her into it.

"Thanks."

"Sure." He cleared his throat. "Now, what's this I hear about an insurance claim?"

"Does someone need help filing one?"

Frank felt somewhat enchanted as she stared up at him. "Um, I understand you offered to help one of our senior citizens—"

"Oh, right. Mrs. Binder. Was there someone else?"

"No." He couldn't believe how clumsy and tongue-tied he'd become.

Cadi seemed to grow uncomfortable under his ogling. The truth was, Frank felt just as awkward, but he couldn't seem to help himself.

She glanced at her watch. "Well, I suppose we should count that money and divvy it up. Are you available?"

Frank bobbed his head in reply and cleared his suddenly parched throat. "Sure."

A teasing grin spread across her face. "Want to hear me whistle just for kicks?"

He drew himself up. "That's not necessary."

"Lucky for you," she retorted, spinning on her heel. "You and your eardrums, that is."

four

"I just have a little business to take care of, and then we can spend the day together."

"But, Daddy," Emily whined, "you said we'd go to the zoo."

"We will. Right after I finish my business."

"I thought it was your day off." Dustin took his spoon and poked at the cereal floating in his bowl.

"Look, you two, I just want to stop at the bank, okay? Then we'll go to the zoo as promised."

"Why can't we go to the bank with you?" Emily said, kneeling on her chair and then throwing her tiny frame into Frank's lap.

"One of these days you're going to miss and land on the floor." He sat his daughter back down in the kitchen chair. "Now, eat your breakfast."

"I don't want to go to Gramma's again," Dustin complained.

Frank blew out a breath of exasperation. His children were not cooperating this morning, and he needed to get to the bank in time to make sure the Disaster Busters didn't swindle an old lady out of her insurance money. Of course, he couldn't tell his kids that. What's more, he was off duty.

"All right. Tell you what. You can come to the bank with me, and then we'll go to the zoo."

"Hooray!" Emily shouted.

Dustin raised his arms, his fists balled in a silent victory cheer.

Pleased with the outcome, both ate their breakfasts, and the ambiance in the kitchen went from gloomy to bright and sunny. Then, while the kids dressed themselves and brushed their teeth, Frank threw together several peanut butter and jelly sandwiches. He placed them into a cooler, along with a cola for himself and juice drinks for the children. Minutes later they all were ready to walk out the front door.

Driving into town, Frank wondered how best to handle the situation at the bank. He couldn't very well come out and accuse anyone without proof, but he hoped his mere presence would deter Cadi and her cohorts from robbing a defenseless, aging widow.

He arrived at the bank after nine and pulled into its adjacent lot. After parking his vehicle, he killed the engine. The kids released their seat belts and hopped out of the sport utility vehicle, following Frank into the financial institution like a pair of ducklings.

Inside, Frank's gaze summed up his surroundings and he spied Cadi seated at a long table in a glass-walled conference room just off of the lobby. The older woman who sat across from her was no doubt Mrs. Binder. He completed his own transaction at the teller window, keeping a watchful eye out; then he moseyed over and rapped on the pane.

Cadi glanced up and waved. Frank entered without further invitation.

"I had personal business here today," he said, his kids still on his heels. "When I saw you ladies, I thought I'd say hello."

Cadi smiled and turned to the woman sitting across the table from her. "This is Sergeant Frank Parker. He's a sheriff's deputy. He was on duty yesterday."

"Nice to meet you, Sergeant." The elderly woman seemed to force her polite smile.

"Frank, this is Mrs. Binder."

"A pleasure, ma'am."

"I phoned the insurance company this morning," Cadi said, "and they faxed over a claim form. Mrs. Binder is filling it out now. The bank manager offered to fax it back once she completes it and signs it."

"It'll never replace my valuables," she lamented, "but it's *something*."

Cadi agreed. "But just remember, Mrs. Binder, the insurance

company said the check could take eight to ten weeks to arrive."

"I'll remember."

Frank decided to jump into the conversation. "And if you have any troubles after you submit your claim, come see me." He pulled out the business card that he'd strategically dropped into the breast pocket of his shirt. The county had cards printed up for all its deputies as folks often liked to know the name and business phone number of the responding officer, particularly in the cases of motor vehicle accidents.

"Thank you," Mrs. Binder said. "I'll remember your offer."

"You do that." *And if she doesn't get her check,* Frank added to himself, *I'll know just who to call.* He glanced at Cadi and grinned.

Moments later, he felt a collective presence behind him. He pivoted and found the four other Disaster Busters members standing behind his kids.

"We're going to the zoo," Emily told them.

"Great day for it," the brunette said. Frank thought he recalled her name being Meg.

"I haven't been to a zoo in ages," a woman with long, brownish-blond hair remarked. She stuck out her right hand to Frank. "I'm Bailey Schmid, and this is my husband, Jeff." She indicated the tall, slim guy at her side.

Frank shook his hand, too.

"I'm Will Angles."

Frank shook the African-American man's hand and noticed the strong, firm grasp despite the man's smaller, slender build.

"Nice to formally meet you all."

"Hey, Cadi," Meg said, "let's go to the zoo after you're finished here. It'll be fun."

"It's a small zoo. You might be disappointed," Frank said. "They've got a couple of bears and a farm animal section, and kids can take pony rides, but, like I said, it's small."

"Sounds fun." Bailey smiled in Dustin's direction. He tucked his chin, obviously overcome by bashfulness.

"Forget the zoo," Cadi replied. "I've got computer work to finish up, and you all promised to return to the explosion site and help several families scrounge up what's left of their belongings."

Frank immediately snapped to attention. He recalled how the last charity organization had looted the devastated properties. He decided to call the office and find out how many deputies would stand guard around the affected neighborhood while people picked through the area.

"We're helping folks this afternoon," Will put in. "I think it might perk us all up if we had some diversion this morning."

"Sure," Meg said. "Even if we spend another night here, it wouldn't be a big deal. We can attend services at Pastor Dremond's church tomorrow morning."

"Spend another night here?" Cadi shook her head. "I'd rather drive home."

"Listen, it's always good to have options," Meg said. "But I say we have a little fun before going back to work this afternoon. I also vote for an overnight stay so we can work right up until it gets dark if we want to and we don't have to worry about being tired and driving back to Waterloo."

"Yeah, Cadi, how 'bout it? The hotel is very comfortable," Bailey chimed in. She turned to Frank. "I never realized Wind Lake is so restful and resortlike."

"More the latter, I'd say. The tourist population is climbing each year."

"So what do you say, Cadi?" Jeff asked.

"I guess I don't care either way."

"Yes!" Will punched the air, acting as if he'd just scored the game's winning touchdown.

Frank chuckled at the man's exuberance.

Meg touched him on the sleeve. "Do you mind telling us how to get to the zoo?"

"Sure, but I still think you'll be disappointed."

"We have fun everywhere we go," Jeff interjected. He stuffed his hands into the pockets of his denim cargo pants and grinned. "We work hard and play hard."

"But Cadi mostly works hard," Meg said.

"Yeah, she's all work and no play," Will added.

"Oh, hush." She waved a hand at them while pointing to a place on the insurance form for Mrs. Binder with the other.

Frank grinned.

"She sounds like my dad," Dustin remarked. "All work. . ."

The growing smile slipped from Frank's face as he regarded his son.

"Well, it's nice that you're going to the zoo with him today, huh?" Meg looked from Dustin to Frank. "Is your wife going on the outing, too?"

"No. I'm not married." Regret and sadness accompanied the answer, although the pain had lessened over the years.

"My mommy's in heaven," Emily told them.

"How marvelous for her," Bailey said, hunkering down so that she was eye level with Emmie. "She's walking the streets of gold with Jesus, but I'll bet you miss her."

Emmie replied with several vigorous nods, but Frank knew she'd been too young to remember. A baby, just over a year old. However, his mother-in-law kept Yolanda's memory alive for the kids.

Frank cleared his throat, hoping for a subject change, although he had to admit to feeling impressed by the candid and empathetic way Bailey responded to his daughter.

"Now about those directions to the zoo," Jeff prompted.

"How 'bout if we just follow you there?" Meg tipped her head and regarded him, waiting for an answer.

"Um, yeah." Frank shrugged. "Sure."

Cadi cleared her throat. "I'm sure we'll find our way. We don't want to keep Sergeant Parker and his kids from their fun."

Frank couldn't help feeling curious when he noticed Cadi's sudden opposition. Was she hiding something? "You're not keeping me. The kids and I are happy to wait a few minutes." He pulled a couple of nickels from his pocket and told Dustin and Emmie to get a treat from the gumball machine by the front doors.

Cadi turned to the elderly woman sitting across from her at the rectangular table. "Mrs. Binder, do you need a ride someplace?"

"Oh, no." She waved a hand at Cadi then dabbed the back of her bluish-white cotton-candy hair. "My gentleman friend is coming to get me." A little pink blush crept up her powdered cheeks. "Don't tell a soul, but he's younger than I am."

Frank chuckled and glanced down at his athletic shoes.

Will made a *tsk-tsk* sound with the side of his mouth. "I'm afraid our Cadi will be pushing ninety-five before she has a *gentleman friend*."

Meg chuckled lightly, Will and Bailey laughed, and Jeff sported a wide grin.

Frank fought against any reaction, knowing it could be misconstrued. Next he saw Cadi's disapproving stare, although he didn't think she possibly could have heard the muttered remark.

"Well, listen, I'm going to take my kids outside," Frank said. "I've got a tan-colored SUV."

"See you in a few minutes." Jeff gave him a mock salute.

As Frank ushered his kids out of the bank, he had to admit he wasn't at all disappointed that the members of the Disaster Busters crew had imposed themselves on their zoo expedition. He thought he might even glean some important information that could come in handy later—like at their criminal trial.

five

Cadi gripped the steering wheel of her minivan until her knuckles turned white. "I know full well what you guys are up to."

Whoops of laughter filled the vehicle, but Cadi tried to block it out and concentrate on her driving. This morning they had unhitched the trailer, and with the hotel manager's permission, they had backed it into a remote corner of the parking lot.

"I told you last night he wasn't married," Meg said, a smile still on her face. "See, I was right—as usual."

"He can't take his eyes off you," Bailey said from the backseat. "It's really a hoot."

"And what a coincidence that he showed up at the bank this morning," Will added.

"He's suspicious of us," Cadi pointed out. "He told me so last night."

"Well, what's he s'posed to do?" Will challenged. "A man's gotta test the water before diving in headfirst."

Cadi rolled her eyes at the analogy. "No, goofball, he's suspicious as in he thinks we're con artists."

"I think you're interested in him, too," Meg said. "I can tell. And we're just helping matters along. This zoo outing is the perfect way for you two to get to know each other."

"I don't want any help with my love life."

"What love life would that be?" Will retorted.

Every nerve in Cadi's body tensed. "Will, you know perfectly well that Darrell and I—"

"Should never have dated in the first place. Yeah, I know that."

She ignored the glib comment. "Look, I don't want another man in my life."

Cadi stopped at a red light and shifted in her seat. She refused to admit that she'd actually dreamed about the handsome deputy last night. *He stood in the misty distance, tall and strong, like a knight in shining armor.*

A car honked, and she jumped. Everyone in the van hooted.

"Like, who could you possibly be daydreaming about?" Jeff chuckled.

Cadi accelerated. "Look, you guys, this isn't funny."

Her friends couldn't have heard her over their laughter.

She tensed all the more.

"I remember you once told me that you wanted to find the right guy and get married," Bailey reminded her.

"I've mentioned that to all my trusted friends, but I was thinking of Darrell when I said it."

"Urrnt." Will made a noise like a game show buzzer. "Wrong choice."

"Okay, I know that now," Cadi admitted, although she also knew she'd have to face Darrell and confirm that their breakup was official. The thought of that confrontation made her cringe.

"Maybe Frank's the right choice," Bailey said. "Find out if he's a believer. Give him a chance. He's definitely interested."

Cadi wanted to argue, but something inside her wanted it to be true. Nevertheless. . .

"I don't have peace about this."

"Oh, that's just because you're nervous." Meg readjusted in her seat belt. "Relax. Enjoy the day."

"Easy for you to say, Miss Matchmaker."

Her friend smiled back in reply. "You'll thank me for this someday."

"Yeah, sure I will."

The SUV up ahead slowed then turned left. Cadi followed it reluctantly, and within moments they drove onto the zoo's surface lot. Cadi pulled her van into the parking space across from the one Frank chose. She opened the door and climbed down from behind the wheel before sliding back the side door by which her friends exited. They traipsed behind Frank and his kids to the front gate where they paid meager entrance fees.

Once inside the zoo, Bailey and Jeff, still newlyweds, walked hand in hand along the stony walkway. Cadi strolled behind them, thinking they made the perfect couple. Their wedding had been an unforgettable collage of music, vows, and celebration of love.

Disappointment settled over her like fog along the Mississippi. She'd always wanted a family of her own, in addition to Aunt Lou. But considering her newly self-imposed condition of "terminally single," Cadi supposed she'd have to abandon the idea of satin and lace and a handsome knight.

She paused by a rough, split-rail fence and gazed inside its circumference. Harnessed ponies stomped and snorted while zoo employees lifted children into the saddles.

Children. Cadi figured that dream had imploded, too—just yesterday when she'd told Darrell good-bye.

Except Darrell had been all wrong for her. Once she'd overheard Darrell's two friends talking. One equated Darrell to patent leather and Cadi to buckskin. Darrell's other buddy remarked that Darrell was a polished gem and Cadi a diamond in the rough. Both had a few chuckles and walked away, never knowing Cadi was standing nearby and had heard every word. At first she took it as a sort of weird compliment, but now she realized Darrell's cronies pointed out what Cadi should have seen all along. There were so many dissimilarities between herself and Darrell.

A man behind her cleared his throat. Cadi started and swung around. Frank Parker and his kids stood there, staring at her. By the curious expressions on their faces, she knew something was amiss.

"What?" She looked from the kids to Frank. "What's wrong?"

"Are you in line for the pony ride or not?" he asked sarcastically. "If not, Dustin and Emily would like to make the next go-round."

Cadi felt her face flame with embarrassment. "Um, yeah. I guess I'll sit this one out." She stepped aside, and the kids ran into the corral.

She turned and leaned her forearms on the wooden fence. Frank did the same.

"So where did your friends take off to?"

"Excuse me?"

"Your friends."

Cadi glanced in all directions. No sight of Will, Meg, Bailey, or Jeff.

"Looks like they ditched me." She expelled a breath, heavy with exasperation. "They think they are so sly. This whole zoo thing is a setup, you know? They couldn't care less about spending the day at the zoo."

"I kind of figured." His gaze never strayed from his children.

Cadi blinked. "You did?"

Frank flicked a glance at her. "I might not be a rocket scientist, but I know a setup when I see it—particularly when it's *me* involved in the setup."

Cadi felt her heart sink out of sheer humiliation. "I'm really sorry. My friends didn't mean to—"

"Don't worry." He gave her a little smile. "I have well-intentioned friends, too." He took a sidestep and faced her. "I put things together on the way here from the bank. You broke up with your boyfriend. They found out I'm single. You're single. Need I say more?"

Cadi felt mortified but managed to shake her head in reply.

"Hey, don't take it so hard. Since my wife died, I have had more 'setups' than I'd care to count."

She could barely breathe. Her friends' practical joke now felt like a punch in the diaphragm.

"Were you two serious?"

"You two—who?" Seconds later, she grasped his meaning. "Oh, me and Darrell." She waved her hand. "No, we weren't serious, although I will confess to having serious delusions of grandeur." Cadi laughed at herself and her silly dreams. "Darrell disapproves of my career choice, and he can't get past it."

"Hmmm. . .so you're a devoted career woman?" Frank's gaze was still plastered to his kids as the horses clomped around in a circle.

"Well, I guess so. I mean, if I want my business to succeed, I have to put time and effort into it. It's just like with anything."

"So, what I'm hearing is that Darrell wasn't worth the time and effort."

"I guess you could say that." Cadi disliked the heartless way it sounded, but for all her hopes and dreams, Frank's summation was right on the mark.

He chuckled so hard that Cadi could feel the fence shake.

"At least you're honest." He stopped short and gave her a sideways glance. "Are you honest, Cadi?"

"I try to be." She frowned, bristling at his implication. "Are you honest?"

"Most of the time."

Cadi put a hand on one hip. "I'm not sure I understand where this conversation is going. Are you telling me you lie?"

Frank straightened. "Not long ago my mother-in-law asked me how I liked her new slacks outfit. She had taken Emmie shopping and found the pantsuit—or whatever you call it—on the bargain rack. I didn't have the heart to tell her I thought it was the ugliest ensemble I ever saw, so I told her she looked real pretty. Guess that's a lie by any measure."

"Maybe. Or maybe it's just saving face with your mother-in-law." She smiled and looked up into Frank's eyes. His dark gaze bore into hers, and her heart skipped a beat. She realized such a reaction had never occurred when she was in Darrell's company.

She averted her gaze, startled by her emotions, and wondered if she should leave the zoo and let her friends find their own way back to the hotel. It would serve them right if she did.

"Nice of you to help Mrs. Binder fill out all those insurance forms this morning."

Cadi sensed what he was getting at. "I'm not swindling senior citizens if that's what you're thinking. The truth is I like helping people."

"Is that why you started Disaster Busters?"

"It's part of the reason." She felt mildly annoyed by the interrogation, although she was familiar with answering for her business. In the past, numerous people had inquired about the hows and whys of starting Disaster Busters. She didn't mind fielding questions when the motives were right. She knew that if she expected people to trust her and her business, she had to be transparent.

But she could tell Frank openly distrusted her. She could read it in his dark eyes.

She fell silent for several long moments and watched the dust plume around the ponies as they clomped in a circle.

At last Cadi decided to take a chance and wear her heart on her sleeve.

"When I was a little girl, my parents, brother, and sister drowned in a flood," she began. "We lived in a small town along the Mississippi River. Actually, the neighborhood in which I grew up isn't even there anymore. It flooded so many times that the government demolished it. Anyway," she said, moving her arm back to the top rail of the fence, "after the tragedy of losing my family, I experienced a slew of bureaucratic horrors. I was in foster care for almost two years until my great-aunt was located and agreed to take custody of me. The entire situation wasn't handled well, from the emergency personnel who saved my life to the court-appointed social workers and presiding judges. When I was old enough to realize just how poorly my case was handled, I vowed to make a difference—to make it easier on victims of natural disasters—so they don't feel like society is kicking them when they're already down."

Frank stared at her, his expression teetering on disbelief.

"If my reply sounds rehearsed, it is to a point," she said, guessing his thoughts. "Sometimes I speak at churches so I can generate financial support for my organization. Disaster

Busters is a business—but it's a ministry, too. Sort of like a pastorate."

He still seemed to be digesting the information.

"Something else about me, too." She smiled. "I'm a born-again Christian. That means—"

"I know what it means. I'm familiar with the biblical term *born-again*. The fact is, I made a decision for Christ when I was a kid."

"Oh." Her reply sounded rather lame to her own ears, but Cadi didn't like the way things were adding up. Frank Parker was a widower and a Christian who could make her heart skip and send her emotions reeling. Maybe her friends were right. Still, there was a gruffness about him that appealed to her about as much as this rough-sawn fence. The man of her dreams was kind and compassionate. Sensitive and caring. Those four words didn't seem to describe Frank Parker. What's more, he didn't appear to be friend material.

"I should be going." Cadi stepped away from the fence. "I'll walk out to the parking lot, and if I don't see my friends, they can either find their own way back to the hotel or call my cell phone."

Before Frank could answer, his children raced over after their ride.

"Daddy, you didn't see me waving to you," the little girl said with a pout.

"I've been talking with Miss Trent, honey. I'm sorry."

"Oh." Emily's gaze slid from her dad to Cadi.

Cadi replied with a guilty smile. She hadn't meant to steal Frank's attention from his children.

Then Dustin looked at Cadi, almost as though he were seeing her for the first time. Was that a glint of enthusiasm in his honey-colored eyes?

"Do you cook dinners like Miss Paige?"

"Or bake cookies like Miss Nicole?" Emily asked with wide, hopeful eyes.

"Paige? Nicole?" Puzzled, Cadi looked at Frank.

"Remember the well-intentioned friends I mentioned? Those two women were, um, setups."

"Ah." Cadi grinned. "And a way to a man's heart is through his stomach."

"Something like that."

She couldn't help a laugh. "Well, Emily," she said, turning to the little girl, "I've got no time for baking. I don't cook, either." She looked at Dustin. "In fact, I'm a terrible cook. I burn everything. Seriously."

Frank looked as though he were holding back a guffaw while the kids scrunched their faces, unable to follow the conversation. At least, Cadi thought, she had quelled any romantic notions he might have.

"Well, have a fun day." She took several steps backward, smiled at the trio, then whirled around and strode to her van as fast as her legs could carry her.

six

"I'm telling you, she's up to no good!"

Adam heaved another sigh. "You have no proof."

"It's a gut feeling—and I trust my gut."

"Sure it's not heartburn?" The pastor swatted at the circling gnats. "Listen, can we talk about this another time? I have a sermon to prepare."

"I realize that—and I'll only keep you a minute." Frank knew from when he used to attend regularly that it was Adam's habit to arrive at church on Saturday evenings and research, rehearse, and pray over his next day's message. Adam had done this for years, which was why Frank chose to meet him here. . .and now.

He glanced around the parking lot, empty except for his SUV, just as Dustin opened the door to the vehicle.

"Dad, tell Emily to be quiet. She won't stop singing."

Emmie's impish voice wafted on the thick summer air. "La-la-la. . ."

"Dad, make her stop. She's plugging her ears. She won't listen to me."

"La-la-la. . ."

"I'll be right there, Dustin."

"Frank, I have my sermon to practice, and you have kids to take home and put to bed."

He swung his gaze back to Adam, who grinned, but Frank had yet to speak his piece.

"I'm telling you, something's up. Cadi's jittery around me; she avoids looking me in the eye." He paused. "She's hiding something."

"I talked to Cadi last night at the barbecue, and she didn't seem jumpy to me. What's more, I spoke with her—"

"Dad!" Dustin's voice cut into the conversation and held a tone of unmistakable aggravation. "She's singing *again*!"

"Okay, son. I'll be there in a sec." Frank turned back to Adam. "Look, about Cadi—"

"She and her team are the real deal, Frank. Go home," the pastor advised. "Relax. Pray about things. We'll talk again tomorrow. I think that when we do you'll agree that Cadi and the Disaster Busters are in Wind Lake to help." An idea lit his gaze. "Hey, come to service, and then you and the kids can come over for lunch. What do you say?"

"Appreciate the offer. I'll consider it." Frank was amazed at the way Adam always worked in the invitation to hear one of his sermons.

"We'll be seeing you later," Adam said as he began to make his way across the almost deserted parking lot. "G'night, kids. Be good for your dad and make Jesus proud."

Frank strode to the SUV and settled the matter between his children, knowing full well that they were exhausted. After the zoo this morning, they went to his parents' condo in a retirement community on the outskirts of town. His folks still worked full-time jobs, but because they were older than fifty-five, they qualified for a condo in the newly constructed retirement center. Both Mom and Dad loved it, as the amenities seemed like luxuries to them after years of living in a century-old farmhouse, but Frank had been sad to see the old place go in order to make room for a strip mall.

"Can't stop progress," Dad had said, and Frank supposed it was true. Besides, his folks' new low-maintenance home meant they had more time to spend with friends and family. This afternoon, for instance, Dustin and Emily splashed and played in the retirement community's indoor pool, under adult supervision. Later, Mom made one of Frank's favorite dinners: spaghetti with meatballs. He ate so much he thought he'd bust, and thankfully, Mom put in a children's video for the kids to watch so the adults could laze around, talk, and allow their meals to digest. Now, however, Dustin and Emily were beyond tired—which accounted for their squabbling.

Pulling alongside the curb in front of the townhouse he rented from his in-laws, Frank parked his vehicle. When the tornado had destroyed his home and killed his wife three years ago, he needed a place to go, and his in-laws just happened to need tenants in the unit adjacent to theirs. So he moved himself and the kids into this two-story place, and he just never bothered to leave. He figured it gave Dustin and Emmie a sense of home, since their grandparents lived right next door. What's more, his mother-in-law, Lois Chayton, ran a day care in her home, which benefited Frank greatly.

"Hi, Gramma! Hi, Grampa!" the kids hollered through the screen door before Frank unlocked their identical front entrance and ushered the pair inside.

He called his own hello to his in-laws before stepping into the sparse living room area. His mother and Lois had tried to spiff up the place by hanging pictures on the wall, and his sister brought over knickknacks, setting them here and there. But the fact remained: Frank didn't give a hoot about decorating his home, although he managed to keep it fairly clean. That was the best he could do, and Lois stepped in and took care of the rest. She knew as well as he did that life hurled issues at him that were much more pressing than housekeeping—issues like taking care of his kids and working sometimes eighty hours a week.

Dustin and Emily took their turns in the shower, and then Frank tucked them into their beds. With each child in his and her respective room and the house now still and silent, Frank moseyed out onto the narrow cement slab of a front porch. He lowered his tired body onto one of the hard plastic lawn chairs and kicked up his feet, setting his athletic shoes on the metal rail.

The night air had a nip to it, but it felt pleasant enough. Refreshing.

He forced himself to relax. His eyelids grew heavy.

"We are so totally lost."

The voice coming from the sidewalk sounded vaguely familiar.

"But that guy said the hotel is this way."

"It's the other way. I'm sure of it."

Frank sat up in time to see two males and two females making their way past his home. Beneath the glow of the streetlamp, he recognized them at once.

"Hey." Frank stood. "Disaster Busters."

They stopped and looked his way.

"It's me, Frank Parker." He stepped off the porch and walked over to them. They greeted him.

"Have you seen Cadi?" Meg asked. "We've been trying to get ahold of her, but either (a) she's turned off her phone because she's, like, really mad at us or (b) her battery's dead or (c) her phone's in her monster purse in which she carries almost everything and she can't hear it ringing."

"If this is multiple choice," Frank said with a grin, "I'm choosing (a)—she's really mad at you." He chuckled in spite of himself.

"So, um, you're on to our matchmaking efforts, huh?" Bailey asked, holding her husband's hand. She looked at her friends. "I guess it was a bad idea."

"Seemed like a good idea at the time," Will retorted; then a broad, mischievous smile lit his expression.

"Except now we're worried about Cadi," Meg informed Frank. "You wouldn't happen to know where she is, would you?"

He shook his head. "She left the zoo right away—as soon as she found out you all took off on her. She mentioned you'd call her cell phone." He rubbed his stubbly jaw. "I don't think she thought the whole setup thing was amusing." He sensed the foursome's embarrassment and discomfort. "If it's any consolation, I took it all in stride."

"Frank, we're sorry if we put you in a bad position," Jeff said, sounding sincere. "Hopefully we'll find Cadi back at the hotel and we can make it up to her somehow. Can you point us in the right direction?"

"What hotel?"

"Wind Lake Inn."

Frank shook his head. "That's on the other side of town. How'd you manage to get so far off course?"

"We were at the explosion site all afternoon, digging through the rubble," Jeff said. "We were able to help one family recover a good number of their possessions."

Frank tried to fight off the doubt and suspicion seeping into his heart.

"Afterward we were invited to eat dinner with a family who will be staying with relatives until their home can be rebuilt," Bailey added. "The Neumanns. Do you know them?"

Frank nodded. "I know them well." He made a mental note to follow up with the Neumanns once the Disaster Busters team left town.

"So after our huge meal," Meg put in, "we all decided the walk back to the hotel would be healthy, and we were told we had a short distance to go, but—"

"But somehow we must have gotten turned around," Will interjected.

Muttering ensued, and he chuckled again.

"This might sound like a stupid question, but did anyone call the hotel and ask for Cadi?"

"We've been calling all day." Meg sighed. "No answer in our room, and all they could tell us is she didn't check out."

"Hmm."

"Frank, are you available to drive us to the hotel?" Jeff asked. "We've been told Wind Lake doesn't have public transportation."

"No, it doesn't."

"Ordinarily we'd never dream of imposing," Bailey added quickly, "but we're exhausted, and I, for one, can't bear the thought of walking across town."

"Sure, I can give you a lift." He supposed his in-laws could watch the kids for a while. "Wait here while I grab my keys."

Cadi sat back on the queen-sized bed in the hotel room and smiled at her laptop. She'd been working all afternoon on creating a Web site for the victims who'd lost everything after the explosion. It had turned out perfectly.

After leaving the zoo this morning, Cadi had returned to the bank and talked with Leslie Pensky, the branch manager. Together they set up an account, and Pastor Dremond agreed to be the signer, overseer, and disperser of the funds. Cadi would give him the signature card tomorrow after the worship service, and the pastor would drop it off at the bank on Monday.

And now, with the Web site up, people everywhere could make a donation.

Lord, I guess it was Your will for me to spend an extra day in Wind Lake.

Cadi glanced at her gold bracelet watch. It was nearly ten o'clock. Where were her friends?

She scooted off the bed and searched for her cell phone, only to realize she'd left it out in the van. No wonder she hadn't heard from them!

Taking strides for the door, the latch clicked, and it opened just as she reached for the handle.

"Where have you been?" Cadi asked as Meg stepped into the room.

"I was just about to ask you the same thing."

Cadi had the good grace to feel chagrinned. "I just realized I left my phone in the van and was headed outside to get it."

"I knew it." Meg snapped her fingers. "We've been trying to get ahold of you all afternoon. I knew you wouldn't purposely ignore us."

"I didn't. Honest. Sorry you couldn't reach me."

"We actually wondered if maybe you'd gone home, but we knew you wouldn't leave us stranded."

"Not a chance, although. . ." Cadi paused. "I thought about it." With a grin she padded to one of the two beds in the room and sat down. "I'll admit that your little prank upset me, but when I left the zoo, I came up with a great idea." She smiled. "I stopped back at the bank, met the branch manager, and set up an account for the explosion victims. Then this afternoon, I created a Web site, just like we planned. Come and look."

Cadi pulled her computer onto her lap and showed Meg the Web pages she'd put together.

"The digital photos Will took this morning before we went to the bank turned out great."

"Absolutely. And they transferred onto my computer and the new Web site with no problems."

Meg sighed. "Well, your Web site is impressive even if your memory isn't." She shook her head. "I'm going to attach that cell phone of yours to idiot strings and make you wear it around your neck."

"That's an idea." Still smiling, Cadi shut down her computer. "So how did things go for all of you this afternoon?"

"We worked as hard as you did. You would have been proud of us."

"I'm always proud of you—my friends."

A wide grin spread across Meg's face before her expression turned serious again. "We made progress, but there is still so much left to do. And so much damage! At one point I had to sob right along with a woman whose cherished family photographs had been destroyed. But then I reminded her that she and her husband are both alive and unhurt, and we both started crying all over again—but crying tears of joy."

"You helped her see the rainbow through the rain. That's important—and that's what Disaster Busters is here for."

Meg nodded and sighed wearily. "When it got too dark to keep searching and sorting, we had dinner with some other volunteers before heading for the hotel—except we somehow got our directions crossed and wound up on the other side of town. Our friendly neighborhood sheriff's deputy gave us a ride."

"Frank?" Cadi stared at her friend, amazed. "How'd you

manage to run into him?"

"Sheer coincidence—if you believe in coincidence, that is."

Cynicism wound its way around Cadi's heart. "He was probably following you all day. He thinks we're lowlife scum who'd rob senior citizens." She stood to ready herself for bed.

"Frank doesn't think ill of us. In fact, he asked all kinds of questions about Disaster Busters while driving us back here."

"He's asking questions because he's suspicious." Cadi searched her overnight bag for her nightshirt and toothbrush. "He's interrogated me at least twice."

"Let him interrogate. We've got nothing to hide."

"I agree. But Frank takes his suspicions way too far."

"Uh-oh. Sounds like you're angry with him." Meg tipped her head. "Or are you angry with us for trying to set you up with Frank?"

"I'm not angry with anybody." Cadi turned her back to Meg, hoping to mask any telltale emotions. "It's just rather insulting to be treated like a thief when you're really trying hard to help other people."

Meg seemed to think it over. "Look," she said at last, "I'll admit Frank has some rough edges." She flopped onto the adjacent bed with its colorful floral spread. "But those edges are probably due to his wife's death. I wonder how it happened."

Cadi strode to the bathroom and closed the door behind her. She told herself she didn't care about Frank Parker or his adorable kids—or how his wife died. But she immediately regretted her harsh attitude. It belied her values, her very being.

Closing her eyes, she prayed for God's peace that passes all understanding. Perhaps by morning her tumultuous feelings would be back under control.

seven

"Daddy, why are you coming to church with us?"

Frank winced. His daughter shouldn't have to ask such a thing. Rather, attending worship services with their dad ought to be a regular event in his kids' lives.

He glanced at Emmie in the rearview mirror of his vehicle. Pigtails in her hair, she sat belted into the backseat, looking darling in her Sunday best, thanks to his mother-in-law's helpful hands. Once more it pained Frank that accompanying his kids to church was such a rarity.

"I'm coming today so I can hear God's Word with you and Dustin. It's the right thing to do. I should have been attending services with you more often."

He spoke from his heart but didn't add that after hearing that the Disaster Busters team would be in church today, he had decided to use his attendance as a great excuse to check them out one more time. He had dual motives, it was true, and he admitted them to God and himself. But at least he was actually on his way to the small, quaint house of worship again, and for the first time there were no tears stinging the backs of his eyes and no lump of sorrow in his throat over having lost Yolanda.

No doubt the reason was because he felt serious about his self-appointed undercover mission. Those Disaster Busters were up to something. Particularly Miss Cadi Trent. Frank just knew it. Why else would he have lost sleep last night thinking about her?

He pulled into the parking lot and slowed his vehicle to a halt. He shut off the engine and climbed from behind the wheel of the SUV, then helped his kids out.

On the way into the building, he greeted several people

he knew and tried to ignore their expressions of shock and surprise at seeing him here again. Inside, he managed to pay little attention to the pity-filled stares. Many in this congregation had known and loved Yolanda, and now they saw him as her unfortunate, lonely widower in desperate need of female companionship.

Ridiculous notion.

Strolling up the center aisle of the sanctuary he bobbed a curt greeting to Paige Dunner, Dustin's Sunday school teacher.

"We missed you today." She waved, and Frank noticed her gray eyes weren't on his son as she spoke. He glimpsed her inviting expression, but he wasn't interested in anything the skinny brunette had to offer.

A few pews later, Dustin halted.

Frank set his hand on his son's shoulder before he could slide in and sit. "Let's go up in front."

"But, Dad, we always sit here with Gramma and Grampa. They'll be getting outa Bible study any minute."

"That's fine, son, but I prefer to sit up front today." Frank had already spotted Cadi's blond hair in the front pew. She might be more hesitant to follow through with any rip-off schemes if she knew he was watching her every move.

"But—"

"Follow me, Dustin."

The boy obeyed, albeit reluctantly. Moments later, Frank and the children slid into the pew directly behind the Disaster Busters. The team greeted him with cordial smiles, but Frank sensed Cadi's unease at once.

She's up to something, all right.

Frank settled into the pew and stared at the back of Cadi's head. He couldn't help noticing that she'd fixed her hair so the usual sassy flips were smoothed under today. He had to admit the style looked more conservative and quite appropriate for Sunday morning service.

His gaze moved down to her slender shoulders concealed

by the teal and black printed jacket she wore.

Then suddenly she turned to hear something one of her friends said, and Frank glimpsed the dangly silver earrings that hung from her lobes. The movement sent a waft of her delicate scent in his direction. She piqued his interest, all right, in more ways than one.

Which makes her even more dangerous, he told himself, folding his arms across his chest.

❧

Cadi wanted to groan out loud when Frank and his kids took occupancy of the wooden pew behind her. She had nothing against those two precious children, but she felt Frank's molten gaze burning into her being. She had a hunch he meant to intimidate her, and she fought to overcome the destructive emotion. After all, no one could intimidate her unless she allowed him to do so.

Besides, Lord, I have nothing to hide. Drawing in a deep breath, she forced herself to relax.

"Dad, did you come to church with us today because of *her*?"

The boy's question reached Cadi's ears. Next she heard Frank's whispered reproof. Meg and Bailey, sitting on either side of her, began to laugh.

"Oh, for pity's sake," she muttered, feeling her friends' shoulders shake in amusement. Couldn't her friends see that Frank viewed them as potential prisoners, not friends?

Lord, please show this distrustful deputy that Disaster Busters is run with integrity. I'd never want to bring shame to Christ's name.

"Thanks again for the ride to the hotel last night," Will said.

Cadi turned in time to see him twist around in the pew and face Frank.

"Glad I could help."

"As you can see, we found Cadi." Will chuckled. "The little workaholic was so intent on building that Web site for victims of Friday's explosion that she forgot her cell phone in the van and never knew we were trying to reach her."

"Web site, huh?"

Cadi thought she could hear the distrust in his tone. She whirled around. "That's right. Web site." But the sight of Frank out of uniform and dressed in a black suit with a periwinkle shirt and coordinating necktie gave her pause. He looked like a model who had just stepped out of the glossy pages of a magazine.

She cleared her throat. "Pastor Dremond is going to announce the site—and explain its purpose."

Before turning back around in the pew, Cadi smiled at the little girl who looked as precious as a baby doll. But not wanting to leave out Frank's son, Cadi reached toward him, palm up. Dustin whacked it. Next she balled her first, and they knocked knuckles.

"What happened to a handshake?" Frank asked facetiously.

"Handshake?" Cadi rolled her eyes. "That was so yesterday."

Frank narrowed his dark gaze at her, but she saw a light of amusement in his brown eyes. She laughed and gave Dustin a mischievous wink.

The boy smiled back at her.

Music suddenly filled the air as the organist and pianist began to play. Cadi turned in her seat just as the choir began filling the loft behind the platform. Minutes later, the ensemble sang a soul-stirring rendition of the hymn "Be Thou My Vision."

Then Pastor Dremond strode to the podium. The coffee-colored suit he wore complemented his reddish brown hair. He read the announcements and moved on to the Web site Cadi created yesterday.

"The Internet has many dangers," he said, "but it can be used for blessings, as well. This site will be a blessing to those in need after Friday's tragedy because it allows those who feel led to do so to donate funds that will in turn be used to provide basic necessities. None of us is rolling in money, but if each of us gives a little, the sum will accumulate into a lot.

And that leads me to my sermon this morning. . . ."

Pastor Dremond began by reading from the Gospel of Luke, chapter twenty-one, beginning in verse one, which illustrated sacrificial giving. "As he looked up, Jesus saw the rich putting their gifts into the temple treasury. He also saw a poor widow put in two very small copper coins. 'I tell you the truth,' he said, 'this poor widow has put in more than all the others. All these people gave their gifts out of their wealth; but she out of her poverty put in all she had to live on.'"

The reverend looked out over the congregation. "Some folks want to hang on to every last coin," he said, "but in the end, they miss out on the best things in life. Likewise, some people don't want to return love and affection or friendship because they're too busy hanging on to their hearts. In a word, they're *afraid* to give."

The pastor asked his congregation to turn in their Bibles to the Gospel of Matthew, chapter ten, verse thirty-nine. "Jesus said, 'Whoever finds his life will lose it, and whoever loses his life for my sake will find it.'"

Again, Pastor Dremond glanced up from his Bible. "I think this verse illustrates how the more we try to hang on to something in this world, the more prone we are to losing it. Including, as Jesus said, our very lives."

The pastor went on to make a few more comparisons and then closed his message with prayer.

When the service ended, members of the congregation crowded around Cadi and inquired about the new Web site. She directed them to her Disaster Busters site, through which they could log on to the Wind Lake Explosion Victims' page. Many thanked her for her service, and Cadi felt blessed, as though she'd truly made a difference in this community.

Once the churchgoers continued on their way, Cadi collected her purse and Bible and headed down the center aisle toward the door.

"You're very innovative, aren't you?"

She recognized the voice at once—but more, she recognized

the cynical tone. Glancing to her right, she spied Frank Parker standing several feet away.

Cadi paused and regarded him. "There's hardly anything innovative about creating a Web page. It's done all the time, and anyone can do it."

"Guess that's my point." He took a few steps forward and narrowed his gaze. "There are a lot of scams on the Internet, and at face value most of them appear on the up-and-up."

"Are you insinuating that I'm trying to scam people using the Web page I created?" Cadi asked indignantly, as heat filled her face and spread down her neck. She glanced around for the reverend. "And do you think Pastor Dremond would be in on such a scam?"

"I merely made a comment, that's all. Do you think you might be overreacting, perhaps out of guilt?"

The remark struck her like a slap across the face. Tears threatened, but she fought to keep them at bay. She drew in a calming breath and held it, knowing she had no good, Christian thing to say to this man.

She brushed past him and left the church. Meg, Bailey, Jeff, and Will were waiting for her in the parking lot next to the van.

"Hey, we've got directions to the Dremonds' house!" Jeff called. His light brown hair was so short it didn't move in the gentle wind.

Cadi pushed strands of her hair off her face. "I'd rather go home. We can pick up some food on the way."

"Fast food compared to a home-cooked meal? The latter has my vote," Will said. "Mrs. Dremond said she prepared pot roast. Mmm-mmm. That's my kind of noonday supper."

As if in reply, Cadi's stomach rumbled. She hadn't eaten breakfast this morning.

"You look upset." Meg peered at her and tilted her head. "What's wrong?"

Cadi momentarily closed her eyes to regain her composure. "Another run-in with our friendly neighborhood sheriff's deputy. He accused me of setting up the Web site so I can steal donations."

"Shut *up*!" Will replied in disbelief. "Maybe you should file some kind of complaint against him. I mean, he has no proof, and his behavior borders on harassment."

Cadi considered it.

"In the meantime, let's drive over to the Dremonds' and eat." Will rubbed his palms together.

"I just want to go home."

"Oh, c'mon, Cadi," Bailey said. "It'll be fun."

"All right. But just remember, we need to get home today. I don't have another change of clothes."

"I'm out of clean clothes, too," Meg said. "Besides, it seems our work is done here."

"I agree, but a few hours at the Dremonds' place won't set us back too far," Jeff reasoned. "It won't take us long to get home."

A moment later the heavy entryway doors of the small country church closed with a bang. Cadi turned in time to see Pastor Dremond exiting the building along with Sergeant Parker and his two children.

"Want me to go talk to him, Cadi?" Will stared in the deputy's direction with a firm set to his jaw. "I'll straighten him out about everything."

"No. Just leave the matter alone. With any luck we'll never see the guy again."

"See you at home in a few minutes!" the reverend called to the Disaster Busters team. Then he shook hands with Frank.

Cadi's gaze met Frank's dark eyes. Tumultuous emotions made her stomach flip while an infinite sadness filled her being. *He thinks I'm out to cheat people.* She looked away and told herself to feel thankful that she'd seen the last of the hypercritical sheriff's deputy. After lunch with the Dremonds, she could retreat to Waterloo and, she hoped, out of his jurisdiction.

eight

The Disaster Busters team piled into the van with Cadi at the wheel. They rode to the Dremonds' single-story ranch-style home, located a mile up the road from the church. With the trailer hitched again to the van, Cadi carefully maneuvered the vehicle up the winding gravel driveway.

All jumped out, and after a hearty welcome from the Dremond kids and Simon, the family's dog, Cadi, Meg, and Bailey offered to help Lindsey Dremond in the kitchen. There wasn't much to do, however, as the trim, dark-haired woman had things under control. So the women chatted and got acquainted while the last of the lunch preparations were made. Then Meg and Bailey went outside to set up the picnic table for the children.

Minutes later, while Cadi carried a porcelain bowl filled with steaming roasted meat, potatoes, carrots, and celery to the dining room table, she heard laughter coming from the next room. She thought she recognized the deep guffaw that certainly didn't sound as if it came from mild-mannered Pastor Dremond.

Oh, Lord, no—not him.

"Cadi, you'll never believe who just arrived with his kids." Meg rushed over to her. "It's that nice officer you like so much."

She had to smile at her friend's sarcastic wit. "Great. I'll look forward to being interrogated while I try to eat."

"Bring it on," Meg said with a smile. "He's outnumbered."

Cadi relented. "True enough."

"Between all of us, maybe we can put that guy's suspicions to rest once and for all."

She nodded in agreement. Her friend made a good point, and with a new perspective, Cadi's nerves felt less jangled.

Until she was seated beside the brawny man at the dinner table. His shoulders were so broad that his arm brushed against Cadi each time he moved.

Pastor Dremond prayed over their food and concluded with a hearty "Amen." Everyone began eating while Lindsey set off to check on the kids and make sure they were behaving outside. She made a quick return and announced that all was well. They didn't mind eating their pot roast under the budding apple blossoms.

"Gorgeous afternoon, isn't it?" Pastor Dremond remarked. "Perfect day in May."

"I love this time of year, but summer is my favorite season." Meg cut into a piece of meat. "Can't wait until it arrives."

"How do you like to spend your summer days?" the pastor inquired. "When you're not responding to disasters, of course."

"Well, I do have a full-time job, and I'm working on my master's degree in Christian counseling. But when I find free time, I play volleyball on a team at church, and Cadi and I enjoy watching the guys play softball."

Cadi gasped at the remark's implication, choking on the iced tea she'd just sipped. Will clapped her between the shoulder blades.

"Gracious me!" A pinkish hue crept into Meg's cheeks. "I, um, didn't mean anything by that comment. We just enjoy the evening games. We mostly sit and talk with our girlfriends in the stands."

Beside her, Frank chuckled.

"We do tend to gab more than we watch the game, I'm afraid," Bailey added.

"My mouth ran ahead of my brain," Meg said apologetically.

"Sure did," Will quipped.

Cadi finished her coughing fit. "Excuse me for getting all choked up."

Chuckles flitted around the table.

"Quite all right," Adam said. "My wife makes strong tea."

Cadi smiled and cast a quick glance in Frank's direction. He was smiling, and he seemed so disarming—so likable—that she wished they could be friends.

"And evening softball games are a favorite pastime of mine, too," the pastor continued. "My oldest son is on a Little League team."

"Awesome," Meg replied, sending a look of apology across the table to Cadi.

She accepted with a smile.

"If I recall, you used to play some softball, Frank."

"That was a long time ago." He shifted in his chair, and his elbow bumped Cadi's. He murmured an apology.

"Your son's close to the right age to join Little League."

"Maybe next year. Dustin has expressed an interest in softball. I guess I could sign him up."

"Great. We can carpool." Pastor Dremond grinned at his wife.

Cadi took a bite of the seasoned beef and savored its rich flavor.

"So, what kind of disasters has this group responded to lately?" Frank asked, changing the subject.

Cadi felt Frank's stare, but with her mouth full, she dared not reply. Instead, she looked across the table at Meg, Jeff, and Bailey, silently urging them to respond.

"You name it, we've been there," Jeff said. "Probably similar, that way, to your line of work, Officer."

"Hmm."

"Feel free to check out our credibility, if you haven't already," Will told him. "We play by the book."

"The Good Book," Bailey added. "Disaster Busters is a Christian organization."

"I ran a check on both the organization and Cadi, and everything came back squeaky clean."

Cadi swallowed. "You ran a check on me?" Stunned, she turned toward him.

"Just doing my job." He peered at her with an unwavering gaze.

Cadi felt more than offended. She was hurt—hurt that someone would dislike and suspect her when all the while her intentions were honorable.

Lindsey cleared her throat. "Well, if you don't mind, I'd prefer if you all didn't exchange disaster stories during lunch. I can barely watch the local news channels. But I'd love to hear what God is doing in your lives."

Bailey replied first, then one by one, they shared miraculous accounts of the Lord's mercy and goodness—all except Frank Parker who, Cadi noticed, didn't contribute to the conversation. What's more, he had the nerve to settle back in his seat and drape his arm over the back of her chair. Cadi, however, refused to be intimidated. The thought of filing a complaint against him, as Will suggested, somehow grew more and more appealing.

After lunch, the reverend cleared the dishes, and his wife served dessert. The children came in, and the boys began begging to play a game of catch with Will, Jeff, Frank, and the pastor. The men declined, but Cadi decided throwing around a ball with the kids sounded better than sitting under Frank's scrutiny a moment longer.

"I'll play with you. In fact, I have a mitt in my van."

"You do?" Frank's son looked awed.

"I'll go get our mitts!" the oldest of the Dremond boys called over his shoulder as he dashed away.

Cadi smiled and turned back to answer Dustin. "Yep, but it's quite by accident. We were in such a hurry to leave Waterloo on Friday that I forgot to remove the box of sports paraphernalia I borrowed from a few friends for the Teen Challenge the church sponsored last Saturday."

"I wondered what was in that box," Will said, kneading his jaw.

"That's right, Cadi. You volunteered to referee, didn't you?"

"Yep. And the kids had a great time."

"Do you have an extra mitt for me?" Dustin asked. "Mine's at home."

"I think there's probably an extra mitt in that box." Cadi smiled at the boy's eager expression.

After excusing herself from the table, Cadi strode outside to her van with the little boys in tow. In spite of the trailer hitched to the van, she managed to retrieve two brown leather mitts and a softball. She handed one glove to Dustin, and in no time a game of catch commenced on the Dremonds' wide, neatly mowed front lawn.

She tossed the ball to one of the Dremond boys. He caught it and threw it to Dustin. Next Dustin pitched the ball to the second Dremond boy who missed the catch and had to go scrambling after it. With ball back in hand, he then threw it to Cadi.

"Dustin, that mitt's too big for you. Pastor Dremond says to use this one."

The deep male voice caused her to make a sharp pivot once she caught the ball. Frank was making his way from the house. He'd shed his suit coat and tie, and now the sleeves of his blue dress shirt were rolled to his elbows. He held a small mitt in one hand.

"That's my old mitt," the oldest Dremond boy said. "You can use it."

Frank made the switch. "Well, as long as I have a mitt, too, I might as well play with you and the kids."

The boys let out a whoop, with Dustin cheering the loudest.

"Sure." Cadi's answer belied the dread she felt inside. But perhaps a simple game of catch would lighten him up and allow Frank to see that she wasn't the villain he assumed.

He stepped in several feet away from Cadi, and Dustin threw the ball to him. Frank caught it easily and tossed it to a Dremond boy. The child, in turn, threw it to Cadi. She hurled it in Frank's direction. Unfortunately, her aim was off and he had to duck before chasing the ball several yards.

Cadi laughed. "Oops. That was an accident. Honest."

He gave her one of his amused scowls.

To his credit, Frank didn't try to retaliate, nor did he pitch the ball over her head so she'd have to run for it in her long, layered skirt and leather flats. But when Dustin missed a catch and scampered to fetch the ball, Frank stepped in closer to Cadi and out of the kids' earshot.

"Know what you are? A pretty little package of trouble, that's what."

"I don't recall asking for your opinion, Officer."

The tart reply caused Frank to grin.

She narrowed her gaze. "Lucky for the both of us, I'm returning to Waterloo and we'll never have to see each other again."

"Unless I have to make an arrest. Waterloo is my department's jurisdiction, too."

Cadi stared at him askance, unsure she understood the connection. "An arrest?"

He nodded. "It's illegal to scam folks off the Internet."

"Of course it is, but I'm not skimming or scamming. And, I must say, you're the biggest bully I've ever met!"

His dark gaze smoldered. "Bully or not, be warned, Cadi Trent. If I find out you're stealing donations off that site you put up on the Internet, I'll make sure the legal ball starts rolling, and I'll gladly see you behind bars."

Cadi was more than taken aback, not so much by the threat, itself, but by the malice dripping off each word. "What did I ever do to make you hate me? I came to Wind Lake to help people after an explosion leveled most of their neighborhood. I was summoned here by the mayor at the request of Adam Dremond. But somehow you decided you could take out all the hatred in your heart on me. Why?"

"Your point is?" His stony expression said her words had little to no affect on him.

Again a wave of incredulity struck her. A second later, she shook her head, realizing how futile it was to plead her innocence to a man who'd already judged her as guilty.

In one smooth motion, she reached out and pulled the

glove off his hand. Next, she moved to retrieve the ball from Dustin.

"I have to go home now," she explained to the boy.

Disappointment dropped over his features as he relinquished the ball. Then he looked over at his dad with questions in his golden brown eyes.

"It was nice playing catch with you." She gave a wave to the other kids in forced politeness. She even managed a smile. After all, they hadn't done anything wrong.

She made her way to the van, climbed in the side door, and tossed the sports gear into the cardboard box filled with other odds and ends. Opening the door on the driver's side, she reached in for her cell phone that she'd mistakenly left inside the vehicle. She refused to walk past Frank again and give him another chance to intimidate her. She'd call Meg on her cell phone and let her know it was time to leave. Meg would inform the others, and Cadi felt certain they'd understand.

She leaned against the side of the vehicle and tried to press in Meg's number, but her hands were shaking so badly from her encounter with Frank that she kept misdialing.

"Everything all right?"

Cadi started as Adam Dremond came around the van.

"Um. . .yeah. Everything's fine," she fibbed. Tears of anger and humiliation pooled in her eyes, and Cadi realized how totally astonished she was by Frank's outright meanness. Her emotions were tangled in knots, and it was all because of *him*. He had her feeling weak-kneed and giddy one minute then horrified and scared the next.

"Your friends are gathering their things and will be out shortly."

Cadi sent the pastor a curious glance.

"We saw you and Frank talking. We couldn't hear what was being said, but judging by your expression, followed by your collection of the ball and glove, we figured something's amiss."

"He threatened to arrest me," Cadi blurted.

"He—what?" A deep frown shadowed the pastor's features.

"He thinks I'm a rip-off artist, and he said he'd 'gladly' see me behind bars." She felt her chin quiver. "I've never even gotten a speeding ticket."

Adam shook his head. "It's not you, Cadi. It's Frank. He's fighting demons from his past. I'm not defending him or his actions. I'm just trying to put things in perspective for you. It's nothing personal against you."

"I beg to differ. Threatening to arrest me is very personal."

An expression of regret settled over the reverend's face. "I'm sorry this happened. And, trust me, Frank won't arrest you. I'll talk to him."

"Well, I have a good mind to contact his superiors."

"Will you give me a chance to speak with him first?"

Cadi mulled over the request then nodded. Pastor Dremond had been kind and gracious from the start, and she was content with leaving the situation in his capable hands.

The rest of the Disaster Busters team showed up, and without a single joke or complaint, they climbed into the van.

"Please thank your wife for a delicious lunch," Cadi said as she slid behind the wheel.

"I will." Pastor Dremond waved good-bye. "Thanks for coming."

After starting up the engine, she pulled away from the curb and pressed her foot against the accelerator. She couldn't leave Wind Lake and its despicable sheriff's deputy fast enough.

nine

"You beat everything, you know that?"

Frank sat back in the sofa and awaited the rest of Adam's scolding, thankful the kids wouldn't be privy to their conversation. Lindsey had taken them to the ice cream parlor in town.

"The least you owe that young woman is an apology."

"I was just doing my job."

"Baloney." Adam ceased his pacing across the carpeting and pulled up a chair. "You were wrong, Frank. Admit it."

"Look, how was I supposed to know that you're the signer on the bank account connected to Cadi's Web site? She could have clarified the situation. Or you could have told me last night when I approached you with my concerns in the church parking lot."

"Had you asked, I would have told you. What I did say was that Cadi isn't up to anything sneaky and underhanded. I knew that—and know that—to be true." Adam looked exasperated as he raked his fingers through his hair. "And if you would have asked Cadi for some specifics, instead of threatening her, I'm sure she would have told you the facts, as well. Your approach was all wrong." He paused and glared at Frank. "You made her cry, you big galoot."

An arrow of regret struck him in the heart.

"The poor girl thinks you're out to get her. She's scared."

He frowned. "Did she say that—that she's scared?"

"She didn't have to!" Adam flung his arms in the air. "It was written all over her face!" He paused. "She's also angry. She threatened to contact your superiors."

"Now that I believe." Frank stood and hardened his inner core. Feminine tears and fears might bend the will of some men, but he happened to think Cadi was a stronger-minded woman than the good pastor made her out to be. Adam's last comment drove that notion home. "Cadi will get over whatever's bothering her, and she can contact whomever she wants. It's her word against mine."

"And yours against mine," Adam reminded him. "My voice will be heard even if you prejudice any higher-ups against Cadi."

Frank knew he had a point since Adam was well-known and respected in the area. His social activism had swayed media personnel and citizens alike.

He turned slowly back around and placed his hands on his hips. He weighed his options.

"Checkmate, my friend." Adam grinned.

Frank raised his hands in surrender. "All right. But don't come whining to me if something goes wrong."

"So you'll apologize to Cadi?"

"I didn't say that."

Adam folded his arms and narrowed his gaze. "You know who you remind me of? My oldest son, Paul. He liked to pull a certain girl's ponytail while they were both at recess. He thought it was fun because he liked her and, at seven years old, he was unsure of how to display such affection." Adam's expression said he was only half amused. "The truth of the matter was, he hurt his classmate each time he pulled her hair."

"You're comparing me to a seven-year-old?" Frank clenched his jaw in irritation. "Thanks a lot."

"You're missing the point. I've watched you all weekend. It seems to me Cadi's gotten under your skin in a way that feels uncomfortable to you. You're lashing out at her, but it's not her fault. You own your emotions."

"Oh, please, spare me the psychoanalysis, okay?"

Adam continued on, undaunted. "Many widowers I counsel tell me they feel guilty for being attracted to other women, even though their wives would have wanted them to remarry and be happy."

Frank moved to leave the living room area and put an end to this whole preposterous subject when Adam, having risen from his chair, sidestepped into Frank's path.

"Consider what I've said, will you? Please?"

"Look, I really don't have time—"

"Make time. Forgiveness—or lack thereof—can steer the soul in the right or wrong direction. The Bible illustrates this truth time and time again."

Frank didn't reply but walked around the pastor and exited the living room. Next he made his way out to the front porch, wishing Lindsey would hurry up and return with the kids so he could collect his two and head for home. He sensed Adam meant well, but Frank didn't care for him or anyone else second-guessing his thoughts and feelings.

Adam strode from the house and stood beside him. "I still think you owe Cadi an apology. You sought her out, Frank. I saw you, and I would have stepped in had I known of your less-than-gentlemanly intentions. I assumed you were getting to know her and quelling your suspicions. Instead, you hurt Cadi, and your abrasiveness was uncalled for."

"Abrasiveness, huh?" He was hardly the steel-wool Brillo-pad guy whom Adam just described. He wasn't a bully, either, as Cadi had accused.

"I have her phone number. Why don't you call her?"

"I know how to find her."

"Okay. I trust you'll contact her, then, and make this right."

Frank glanced at Adam. "I'll think it over, but I'm not making promises."

Adam didn't reply. The subject was dropped. A few minutes went by and small talk ensued.

Sometime later, Lindsey finally pulled the large van into the driveway. The children jumped out, and Frank steered Dustin and Emmie into his SUV.

He drove home, listening to his children prattle on about how much fun they had this afternoon. Dustin mentioned Cadi and said he wished she would have played ball longer.

Frank's heart wrenched, and he battled against everything Adam said to him. But it was true: Frank had sought out Cadi for dubious reasons.

So now what do I do? He hated the thought of swallowing his pride and apologizing. There was a chance, after all, he still could be right about Disaster Busters.

Pushing the matter from his mind, he chose to deal with it later.

He pulled into the driveway, and once inside the house, he prompted Dustin and Emily to shower, get their pajamas on, and brush their teeth. He was met by a whiny resistance from his daughter and a few complaints from his son, but by nine o'clock, both kids were in bed for the night.

Frank flipped on the TV and tuned in to a local cable news show. Then he collapsed into the soft, black leather sofa and pulled the Sunday newspaper onto his lap. He had just found the sports section when Dustin padded into the living room.

"Dad?"

"Hmm?" He glanced up from the newspaper. "What is it, son?"

Dustin hedged but then stepped forward. "Dad, how come you were mean to Cadi?"

"What are you talking about?" Frank saw his son flinch at the harsh tone, and he softened it at once. "When was I mean to Cadi?"

"When we were playing ball. I heard you say you'd be happy if she was locked up in jail. You scared her."

"Oh, I was just kidding around," Frank fibbed for his son's sake. "Cadi just got mad at me, that's all."

"But I saw her face. It turned a funny color—like when Emmie was sick—and then she took her stuff and went home."

"Don't worry, son. I didn't scare Cadi. In fact, she had some choice words for me, too. Everything's fine." Frank fought the aggravation rising inside of him. He felt like accusing the Dremonds of somehow brainwashing his kid, but he knew no such thing occurred—unless Lindsay had mentioned the situation when she took the children for ice cream.

"Did Mrs. Dremond say that I scared Cadi?"

The look of surprise, followed by the shake of Dustin's head, told Frank the boy hadn't been influenced.

"Well, look, Cadi's a grown woman. She can handle it." He pulled Dustin in beside him on the couch and kept an arm around his shoulders.

"I like Cadi," the boy said.

"That's nice." Frank felt his jaw tense.

"She's pretty." Dustin twisted around to peer up at Frank. "Do you think she's pretty, Dad?"

"Sure." He hoped his reply sounded uninterested.

"Maybe you should ask her on a date."

He shook his head. "Dustin—"

"Dad," he said emphatically, crawling up on his knees to be face-to-face with Frank, "*she's got her own mitt.*"

"Oh, well, in that case. . ." He sent a glance sky-rocketing and chuckled.

"Da–ad." Dustin's lips curved downward and his golden-brown eyes glimmered with unshed irritation.

"I'm not laughing at you, son," Frank quickly put in. "I'm grateful for your opinion. I'll think about it, all right?"

"Okay." The eight-year-old appeared satisfied for the time being and took off up the steps and back to bed.

Alone in the living room, Frank had his own private laugh. *Typical boy. A pretty lady plays catch with him and right away he thinks I should ask her on a date. What a hoot. Funnier yet is that Cadi would never go out with me. She probably rues the day we met.*

He recalled her question: *"What did I ever do to make you hate me?"*

Remorse stung his very soul. He opened the sports page and tried to shake off the feeling, but it continued. Could he really have been so wrong about her? Was her work genuine, as she maintained? Or was Cadi just the best liar on the planet? Of course, Adam supported her, and he wasn't easily fooled. Or was he?

Frank decided to do some more digging on her and the members of the Disaster Busters. If the info he found—or didn't find—proved he'd been wrong about her, he'd apologize. But only then!

❧

"You can't be serious."

Cadi sent Meg a sideways glance as she drove home. It had been nearly eighty degrees today and she and Meg, along with a host of teenagers from church, had washed cars, vans, and trucks all afternoon. The event was a fund-raiser for the teen mission team and they'd raised quite a bit of cash, but now Cadi felt the effects of her labor. Worse, she'd picked a poor time to inform Meg of her decision to reconcile with Darrell.

"That guy is the rudest and most condescending man I've ever met. What's more, he's conceited."

"He knows his faults. He's working on them. Besides," Cadi said, "I can think of worse rude and condescending men." Frank Parker's swarthy image flitted across her mind.

"You know, Meg, I've come to realize I didn't give things between Darrell and me a chance. Darrell and I talked on the phone several times this week, and I decided to actually work at our relationship now. Maybe my influence will somehow make Darrell a better person. He said I'm like a reality check for him."

Meg didn't seem swayed in the least. "You're making a huge mistake, but it's your life."

Cadi didn't appreciate how Meg dismissed the subject so quickly. On the other hand, they'd had this discussion before and Meg never had cared for Darrell.

"Let me ask you this," Meg blurted. "Does he make your knees weak and your heart sing?"

Again, the image of Frank Parker loomed in Cadi's memory. "That's ridiculous. You can't trust emotions when making important decisions about a relationship. Emotions can be totally deceiving."

"Maybe, but when my knees get weak and my heart sings,

I'll know I've met the man of my dreams."

"Well, just to warn you, every warm and fuzzy emotion went off while I was near that deputy last weekend, and he was the meanest person I've encountered in a very long while."

"So you admit your attraction to him, eh?" Meg turned in her seat despite the seat belt across her slim body. "Is that why you're getting back together with Darrell? You're fighting your feelings for Deputy Parker?"

"No and no." Cadi regretted her sudden harsh tone. She softened it at once. "I mean, of course I'm not."

"Look, I'm the first to agree that last weekend was full of unfortunate experiences for you, but I don't think the guy is, as you say, 'mean.' I think there's a lot of misunderstanding going around." Meg paused. "While you were out playing ball with the kids last Sunday, Pastor Dremond told us about that bogus charity organization that came to Wind Lake a few years ago."

"What are you talking about? What bogus charity organization?" Cadi ran a hand through her hair after stopping for a red light.

"You mean you don't know? I assumed Pastor Dremond told you long before he ever mentioned those creeps to us."

"No, this is the first time I'm hearing about it."

"Well, apparently several men said they were in town to help after a bad storm, but they looted damaged property and stole jewelry and other valuables. In short, they were a bunch of thieves."

"Hmm." Things started making sense to Cadi. "No wonder Sergeant Parker distrusted us from the start." She shook her head. "Why weren't we told about this?"

Meg rotated her shoulders in uncertainty. "I thought you knew about it already, and I guess no one else in Wind Lake was suspicious of us except for Frank. While he was outside playing ball with you and the boys, Will told Pastor Desmond about Frank's interrogating you. That's when the pastor told us about the fake charity group." Her tone of voice softened.

"He also said Frank's been through a lot these past few years."

Cadi refused to feel sorry for the guy. "I'm sure he has, but that fact doesn't excuse bad behavior."

"I agree, but—"

Cadi didn't want to hear any "buts." She wanted to forget about it—and about Frank Parker.

She glanced at her watch as the light turned green. "I've got to hurry and drop you off and get home so I can shower and change. Darrell is taking me to his older brother's thirtieth birthday party tonight. He's picking me up at six. I'm going to have to hurry."

Cadi watched as her best friend folded her arms across her chest and pressed her lips together in taut disapproval. What's more, Meg didn't utter another word the rest of the way to her apartment.

ten

Balloons of every color streamed from the ceiling along with a banner that read OVER THE HILL. Cadi thought the black-lettered proclamation was premature for Darrell's older brother; however, she agreed that turning thirty was a benchmark in a person's life, and she couldn't help wondering where she'd be in five years. Would she be married? Have children?

She smoothed down the multicolored challis split skirt she wore beneath a matching top. She chanced a look at Darrell, who stood beside her, polished and suave from the top of his honey-colored hair to the tips of his expensive leather loafers. Again she wondered what her life would be like in the future, and suddenly, she couldn't quite imagine herself married and sipping her morning coffee with him.

He smiled down at her, and Cadi pushed out a grin before glancing around the crowded living room. People were talking and laughing, having a good time. She, too, had enjoyed talking to different folks for most of the night, and she'd sung choruses of "Happy Birthday to You" with them, filling the entire ranch-style home with merriment.

"Having fun?" Darrell moved closer and slipped his arm around her waist. Cadi tensed. Why did his touch feel unwelcome? All evening she'd thought about what Meg said earlier, and she wished her knees would weaken and her heart would "sing" whenever Darrell was near. Instead, Cadi's heart seemed to recoil.

Lord, what's wrong with me?

Cadi immediately sensed her heavenly Father's reply. Had she prayed about getting back together with Darrell? No. So what was she trying to prove? That she wasn't a sap for a certain sheriff's deputy who'd rather see her in jail than on the other side of the table from him in an upscale Italian restaurant?

Practical. Love is practical, she reminded herself.

She turned and regarded Darrell once more, but this time she caught him staring off in the distance. She traced his line of vision across the room to a petite blond in a slinky black dress. The woman's long hair hung to her waist.

Cadi cleared her throat and nudged him with her elbow.

Darrell looked down at her. "You should grow your hair long," he muttered after flashing the other woman a cosmopolitan smile.

A myriad of emotions filled Cadi's heart, the foremost being irritation. "I *should*, huh? You don't like my hair?"

"Oh, listen, I didn't mean anything by it. Let's not argue. We've just gotten through all that other nonsense."

"Nonsense?" Cadi tipped her head expectantly. "What nonsense?"

He gave her a patronizing grin. "All our broken dates because of your business."

"Are you blaming me?" Cadi felt her face begin to flame. "Darrell, for your information—"

"Shh." He kissed the side of her head, and Cadi resisted the urge to slap him away. "We'll talk about it later."

Cadi bristled, and the overwhelming notion that reconciliation with Darrell was an impossibility filled her being. The man of her dreams wouldn't want to make her something she wasn't.

Grow my hair long. Yeah, right, she fumed.

She watched as Darrell stood ogling the blond across the room. The man of her dreams wouldn't have roving eyes, either!

Although she'd vowed to give their relationship a second chance, she never said she'd change her appearance for him simply because he admired a certain feature on another woman. Truth be told, his wandering gaze wasn't exactly a new practice. But when she'd agreed to work at their relationship, Darrell had promised to kiss his playboy ways good-bye forever.

So much for Darrell keeping his end of the bargain.

Meg was right. I should have listened. What was I thinking?

A sense of betrayal gripped her. Disgusted, she shrugged out of Darrell's hold. She felt the need to get away from him, so she strolled over to a group of young women chatting by the porch door.

Keep calm, she told herself. *Darrell and I can discuss this matter in private.*

She recognized Liza Redelli from church and sat down in the maple dining room chair beside her. Out of the corner of her eye, Cadi watched Darrell head for the shapely blond.

In that moment, Cadi knew without a doubt that she and Darrell would never be a couple.

"Hi, Cadi." Liza turned her way. "Good to see you. What's new?"

Cadi swallowed her emotions.

"Hi, Liza." They conversed for a few minutes and, before long, Cadi was overcome by a fierce determination to find another ride home. She'd come with Darrell, but there would be blizzards in Bermuda before she climbed into his sports car tonight and allowed him to behave as if nothing had happened again.

She glanced his way, and as if in affirmation, she spied him and the other woman steeped in what appeared to be an intimate chat. Chances were he'd never know Cadi even left the party.

"Liza, I need a ride home," she blurted. "Can you give me a lift?"

Liza shook her head, and her nut brown hair brushed against her plump shoulders. "I came with three other people in a compact car. There's no room for one more."

"Okay. I understand. Thanks anyway." Cadi weighed her options.

"I'll give you a lift home."

The voice caused Cadi to turn in her chair. There, behind her, stood Ross Hinshaw. A heavyset guy with nondescript brown hair and acne lesions on his chin, it appeared Ross hadn't changed a lot physically since Cadi last saw him. She'd gone to high school with him, and although he wasn't a Christian back then, she remembered him as a nice enough guy.

"I'm actually leaving in a few minutes," he said. "Let me just tell my buddy. He's going to another party after this one."

"Great. Thanks." She gave him a smile, noticing a slight dip in his gait as he walked away. She wondered if he had knee problems or perhaps a bad back.

In either case, Cadi just felt grateful for the ride home.

He returned a few minutes later, and they walked outside to his shiny black pickup.

"Didn't you come here tonight with Darrell Barclay?" Ross asked as he put the transmission into gear.

"Yes, but—well, it was a mistake. That's all I can say about the situation."

"Oh yeah? His loss might be my gain." Ross chuckled.

Cadi gave him a curious glance and noticed his lopsided grin as they drove under the glow of a streetlight. The comment made her nervous, but she brushed it off by telling herself Ross meant it as a backhanded compliment, nothing more.

"You still live in that old Victorian house on Daisy Drive?"

"Yes. With my aunt. You've got a good memory."

"Yeah, well, my folks still live about half a mile from there."

Cadi recalled the general vicinity of the neighborhood in which Ross grew up. "I hope you don't have to drive too far out of your way."

"Naw, it's okay."

"I appreciate the ride home." She chose her words with care so as not to encourage him in any way. "What have you been doing since graduation from high school? Did you go to college?"

"Some."

As Ross started talking, Cadi noticed something odd about the way he pronounced many of his words. He didn't exactly slur them, but Cadi had the impression something wasn't right.

"Are you feeling okay?" she asked as Ross pulled onto the expressway.

"I'm fine." He cracked his window then turned up the vehicle's stereo system. Heavy metal music filled the truck's cab.

Ross lit a cigarette, and Cadi wondered if she wouldn't have been better off going home with Darrell—even with his wandering eyes and flirty ways.

"What about you? What do you do for a living? I heard you were a nurse or something."

"An EMT. Emergency medical technician." Cadi had to practically shout over the blaring noise. Worse, the vulgar lyrics pulsing from the stereo made her cringe. "Can we turn this down a little?"

"Sure." Ross obliged.

Cadi expelled a breath of relief.

"Where you working?"

She began explaining about her business, Disaster Busters, how it functioned, and her position, but soon she realized that Ross was driving at an increasingly excessive speed. They'd turned off the expressway and were traveling a remote stretch of highway that led into Waterloo.

The truck's tires squealed as the vehicle rounded a curve.

Stay calm. Twenty minutes, tops, and I'll be home, Cadi thought in an attempt to placate herself. Then, several miles later, she saw the familiar bend in the road.

"Hey, Ross, you might want to slow down. I see Suicide Hill up ahead."

"Suicide Hill." He laughed and lit another cigarette. "It's not dangerous. I've driven this road a million times. Relax. I'm in control." He turned and grinned at her.

"But. . .you're going way too fast!"

Just as Cadi finished the last syllable, the truck went onto the shoulder. Dirt and gravel pelted the vehicle's underbody. Ross snapped to attention and yanked on the steering wheel, making a sharp left. His correction sent the truck careening over the centerline. Headlights from an oncoming car flashed through the windshield.

"Ross, watch out!" Cadi screamed.

He fought for control as the truck fishtailed. Again the tires screeched beneath them. Then another jerk on the wheel and the truck sailed down a hill. It sped across a yard before slamming head-on into a wooden stockade fence. The air bag in front of Cadi deployed on impact, ramming into her chest and face, stealing her breath away.

She gasped for air and battled to inhale. Then, before she could utter a prayer, she submerged into total darkness.

❧

"What do we have here, Marty?" Using his Maglite, Frank surveyed the crash scene from the side of the road.

"Other than the obvious, I'm not sure yet," the other officer replied. "A passerby made the 911 call. Fire truck and ambulance are on the way."

"Victims? Survivors?"

"Like I said, I don't know. I just arrived on the scene myself."

Muted moans of distress in the near distance spurred Frank and his colleague down the hill.

"Careful. There might be downed wires, Marty."

"I'll keep a lookout for 'em."

Following the tire tracks into the undeveloped acreage, they stumbled upon a man lying prostrate on the damp ground, groaning in agony.

Marty bent to assist him.

Frank continued his survey of the area. "Anyone else in the truck?" he asked the injured man.

"Yeah, but I think she's dead. And—and she was driving. It wasn't me. She was driving."

Frank set off toward the mangled pickup. He mentally braced himself for the sight he might find. He'd seen it before, and it wasn't pretty. Never was.

A patch of brightly colored fabric caught his eye, and several strides later, he found a woman heaped on the ground near the rear of the truck. Her position, closer to the passenger side than the driver's, raised questions in his mind about who had really been at the wheel when the truck crashed.

Arias of sirens from oncoming emergency vehicles sang in the distance. Meanwhile, Frank hunkered down beside the female and found a pulse.

Good news.

He searched her swollen, bloodied face and red-stained blond hair. A slow recognition seeped its way into his thoughts, but he figured he had to be imagining things.

He checked the woman for obvious fractures and found none, but her height and body shape matched that of a certain Disaster Buster he'd recently met—and couldn't seem to forget.

Again, he shone his light into her face. By the looks of it, her nose was broken.

"Cadi?" He set his hand on her shoulder to prevent her from moving in case of a head, neck, or spinal cord injury. "Cadi, is that you? Can you hear me?"

Her eyes fluttered open, and he glimpsed their blue depths. He knew without a doubt it was her.

"Oh, it's you."

Her less-than-enthusiastic reaction was like a knife in his heart.

She stirred.

"Be still. The paramedics will be here in a few minutes."

"I need to sit up. I—I can't breathe."

Frank tried to stop her from moving, but she was in obvious distress. At last he propped her up the safest way he knew how and hoped her injuries weren't worse than they appeared.

"That's better," she panted. "I felt like I was suffocating."

"Stay still, Cadi. You might have internal injuries or broken bones."

"I managed to crawl out of the truck by myself and make my way this far."

Frank felt both impressed and amused. "Do me a favor and stay still, okay?"

"Or what? You'll arrest me?" She tried to stand.

"Cadi, you're hurt. Let's call a truce so I can help you."

She replied with a half groan and half cry.

"Let me help you."

She didn't protest further, and Frank tried to make her comfortable. The seconds passing seemed like hours. He couldn't imagine what was taking the paramedics so long to arrive.

Cadi began to struggle again.

"Take it easy."

"Is the truck going to blow up?"

"I doubt it." Frank shined his flashlight on the mangled vehicle. He detected no signs of danger.

"I heard Ross say—say the truck was going to blow up. I was so freaked out."

Incensed, Frank silently summed up the situation. *So the guy took off running and left Cadi inside—what a jerk.*

"Is he okay? Ross? Is he hurt?"

His anger toward the man pulled Frank's nerves taut. "Don't fret over him. He's not worth the energy, Cadi. Trust me."

"I fret about everybody. I've made helping others my—my whole life."

"Relax, Cadi. You don't owe me any explanations."

She quieted.

"That's better."

"Why aren't you telling me about—about Ross? Was he killed? I want the truth."

"He's alive." Frank directed his flashlight off into the distance. He saw that Marty had helped the guy to his feet. They were slowly making their way up the hill. "In fact, my guess is your boyfriend will make a full recovery."

Frank wanted to add that the guy had left her for dead—

that he'd lied about which one of them was driving when the crash occurred. But he refused to upset Cadi further. He was outraged, however, that she cared about someone so obviously self-absorbed. Was this her boyfriend? The one she broke up with? Or was this someone new? Either way, it was obvious to Frank that she sure knew how to pick the losers.

Then, suddenly, his rationale did a 180-degree turn. He felt like King David when the prophet Nathan proclaimed, "You are the man."

Contrition enveloped him. If any mutual attraction had existed last weekend, it made Frank little better than any other "loser" in Cadi's life. What's more, his brutish behavior clinched the title for him.

Loser.

The paramedic squad and fire truck finally arrived, and the red and blue lights illuminated the starlit night.

"Cadi, everything's going to be all right. I promise you."

She caught his wrist and murmured something, but with all the approaching noise, Frank couldn't make it out.

"Say it again; I didn't hear you." He knelt closer.

"Ross is not my—my boyfriend," she said with a labored breath.

"Glad to hear it." *In more ways than one,* Frank added to himself.

"Will you help me stand?" She began to struggle.

"Good grief, Cadi. Don't move any more. You might be doing more damage to yourself."

"But I can't breathe."

"Relax." He shrugged out of his lightweight jacket and carefully placed it behind her head and over his knee, propping her even higher. "Is that better?"

"A little."

He brushed the stained and matted hair off her face. "Just relax," he repeated.

In the distance, the emergency personnel gathered their gear and headed toward them.

"Frank?" Cadi's weakening voice reached his ears. The way she said his name did something crazy to his insides.

"What is it?" In that moment, he thought he'd do just about anything to help her.

"I—I hate to tell you this, but—"

"Tell me what?"

"I—I..."

Frank wondered if a confession of some sort was on the way. "What is it, Cadi?"

"I—I think I'm going to be sick!"

eleven

The hospital room's stark ceiling blurred before it came into focus again. Cadi blinked and fought the effects of the pain medication she'd been given. Over the course of the last several hours, she'd had every X-ray imaginable, and the worst of her injuries seemed to be a broken nose and a fractured rib as well as multiple bumps and bruises.

She touched the swollen and throbbing center of her face. The specialist on call had finished packing and setting her broken nose; then he'd spoken about the possibility of plastic surgery.

The entire situation seemed so surreal. Had Frank really been the responding officer, or had she dreamed up their verbal exchange? She had almost convinced herself that the latter was true. After all, Frank Parker thought she was a swindler and said he'd gladly see her behind bars. But it was a totally different man—a sort of hero—who had knelt over her and tried to help her tonight.

Cadi's eyelids grew heavy and fluttered shut. She allowed the fantasy of her knight in shining armor to play out in her head. She knew the morphine had a lot to do with her delusional state, but she was too exhausted to fight it.

Minutes later, she heard the glass exam room doors slide open then close again. She sensed a presence and opened her eyes. The dream vanished, and she watched in chagrined awe as the very object of her thoughts neared her hospital bed. She blinked, wondering if she'd somehow conjured him up.

"Hi."

"Hi."

"Mind if I ask you a few questions?"

"Sure, I—I guess not." She struggled to sit up but found it

hurt too much. She then maneuvered the head of the bed to more of an upright position. Frank quickened his strides and assisted her.

"I would have come in to talk to you sooner," he said, "but I, um, had to shower and change my uniform."

"Oh?" Cadi didn't understand his meaning at first and decided that in his spotless beige shirt and green trousers, he looked like a real-life version of the fabled rugged, tall-dark-and-handsome hero.

And that's when she realized the unfortunate reason for his just-pressed appearance.

She closed her eyes and winced. "Oh, I'm so sorry—"

"You couldn't help it."

She peeked at him and found him leaning his muscular forearms on the side rail. His presence seemed too close for comfort.

He smiled and shook his head. "Girl, you look like you were in a boxing match and lost."

"Thanks a lot." Cadi almost laughed, but the pain shooting through her body stopped her cold. "No jokes." She wrapped her arms around her midsection.

"Fair enough."

Cadi marveled at how disarming Frank was when he smiled. But soon the amusement disappeared from his face.

He glanced at his clasped hands, and she thought his fingers looked strong and capable. "Cadi," he said gravely, "I have my assumptions, but I need to hear it from you. Were you driving that pickup tonight?"

He looked back up at her, and his dark gaze bore right into her.

"No, I wasn't driving." She wished she didn't feel so vulnerable. She hiked up the white sheet covering her gown-clad body and tucked it under her arms. "Ross was driving."

"He swears up and down that it was you."

Cadi swallowed hard and willed away the tears of indignation forming behind her eyes. "Well, you already think I steal and cheat disaster victims, so I'm sure you think I'm a liar now, too."

"Slow down." He placed his hand over her forearm. "I'm not thinking the worst of you, all right?"

When he paused, Cadi glanced his way.

"The fact is, I thought about calling you and apologizing for my boorish actions last weekend, but I sort of lost my nerve."

Cadi arched one bruised brow. "You? Lost your nerve?"

She watched him wrestle with a grin. "Believe it or not, us macho guys have fragile egos."

Cadi laughed and groaned in agony at the same time. "Frank, that was *so* not nice!"

"I wasn't trying to be funny." He smiled in spite of himself.

She caught her breath then gave him a withering glance.

"Seriously," he said, his tone resonating with sincerity, "I'm sorry I acted like—to use Adam's words—'a big galoot.'"

So Pastor Dremond spoke to him just as he promised.

"I hope you can forgive me."

"I can—and I do." It certainly wasn't difficult while he was being so charming.

"Good."

She stared at him, trying to figure out this man. She recalled Pastor Dremond saying Frank wrestled with something from his past. Was it more than his wife's death?

"I'd rather have you as a friend than a foe," she murmured.

"Ditto."

The light in his eyes made her heart melt.

"But, for now, let's get back to business. For the record, I'm going to ask you again: Were you driving?"

"No."

"Were you drinking tonight?"

Cadi gasped then winced at the lightning bolting through her ribcage. "I don't drink," she managed through gritted teeth.

"Did you know Ross was intoxicated when you got into the

truck with him tonight?"

Cadi gaped at the question. "He was intoxicated?"

"I'll take that as a no." Frank straightened. "How do you know this guy?"

"I don't really know him. I mean, I know who he is because we went to high school together. I was at a birthday party and needed a ride home. Ross offered, and I accepted."

"Cadi, he was drunk." Frank leaned in again.

"I had no clue. There was no alcohol served at the party. The Barclays are Christians who don't believe in celebrating with liquor, so it never occurred to me that Ross—"

"Okay, I get the picture." Frank stood to his full height. "How'd you get to the party?"

She hedged, not wanting Frank to know the many wrong choices she'd made in the past seven days. But then again, if her answer was too vague, he might find grounds to mistrust her again.

She decided to shoot straight from the hip. "Darrell picked me up."

"Darrell. . ."

She could see his mental gears turning.

"Is that the guy you broke up with?"

"Yes." She gazed up at the ceiling tiles again and chastised herself for not heeding Meg's warnings about Darrell. "I thought we could reconcile, but things will never work between us. If that fact wasn't obvious to me before, it certainly was tonight."

"Hmm, and how did you come to that conclusion?"

"His roving eyes."

"Ah. That'll do it."

"And when Darrell became engrossed in the company of another woman—whose long blond hair is not that impressive, if you ask me—I decided to find my own way home." She looked at Frank. "You know the rest of the story."

She watched her explanation play across his shadowy features. He seemed to ponder the logic, or lack thereof. "Are you finally through with this guy now, or what?"

She couldn't help a grin. "Is this on or off the record?"

Frank had the good grace to look embarrassed for asking. "Off."

"We're really through."

"Good." Frank gave her a nod of approval.

"Good?" Cadi felt a tad bewildered by his emphatic reply.

"Well, look. . ." He cleared his throat. "I'll give Marty, the officer in charge, all the information. It's customary for us to do an investigation, particularly since Ross was intoxicated when he got behind the wheel. But I think you should know that I'm requesting to be taken off this case after tonight."

"Why?" She stared into his face, almost losing herself in the depths of his velvety brown eyes. "Am I in trouble?"

He stared back at her. "No, but. . ." He paused. "I think maybe I am."

"Oh?" She hadn't filed any complaints.

She watched in puzzlement as a grin spread across his face.

"I feel like I'm too close to this case, personally, to be objective."

The explanation made sense.

"I need to get going." After a parting smile, he strode toward the door then stopped. "Oh, and your aunt is anxious to see you. I apologize for keeping her waiting, but I needed to speak with you first. All the evidence backs up your story and. . . Cadi?"

"Yes?"

"Just to warn you, Ross Hinshaw is going to jail. His recklessness could have killed him, you, and countless others on the road tonight."

"You're right." The realization that so many lives could have been lost gave Cadi a jolt, and in that moment, she gleaned a sliver of insight into Frank's world. Obviously he often dealt with the worst side of humanity. Little wonder that he'd developed such a granitelike demeanor.

Except she'd glimpsed his softer side, too—like when his

children were around and in the way he'd tried to help her tonight.

"Thanks, Frank. Thanks for everything."

He replied with a smile and an amiable wink then left the room.

੩

Except for sending her flowers and talking to her on the phone a couple of times, Frank refrained from contacting Cadi. Instead, he allowed the first few weeks of June to pass before entertaining thoughts of a bona fide courtship. He figured she needed time to get over her failed romance and recover from her injuries before he approached her and asked her out.

Still, he kept himself abreast of the goings-on in her life by logging on to the Disaster Busters Web site almost daily. He read Cadi's blog, and it gave him a clearer view of her character. In a word, she impressed him. He read her account of the car crash and her recent campaign against drunk drivers. He silently applauded her for taking action, and each time he saw Cadi's photograph on the site—and her blue eyes and smiling face—the notion of dating her made his mouth go dry.

Did he have time to cultivate a relationship? Could he make time? What would the kids think? What would his parents and in-laws think? Would they approve of Cadi? He hated the thought of what might happen if they didn't. Losing Yolanda had been devastating enough, and Frank didn't think that he or any of his family members had the energy for more drama.

So, did he dare set off on this romantic pursuit? He had a hunch Cadi wouldn't be opposed to it. But what if things wouldn't work out? She was a career woman and a crusader. He was a workaholic with two kids.

Maybe he shouldn't bother.

Frank expelled an audible sigh. He stood from the kitchen table where he'd been sitting, contemplating. He stretched and glanced out the patio doors and into the backyard where Dustin and Emmie played with their friends. Convinced all was well outside, he moseyed over to the sink and washed the supper dishes while rehashing the situation over in his mind.

Before long, his children's friends had gone home, the kitchen was clean, and dusk had settled. Frank called the kids into the house, and once they were washed up and in their pajamas, they settled on the couch to watch their favorite TV shows. Frank sat between them, one arm around each child. He relished quality time like this, so when a nature program came on one of the cable channels, he allowed the two to stay up late and enjoy it.

Then it was time for the local news.

"Okay, time for bed." Frank stood and stretched.

The kids moaned in unison.

"No arguments." He was just about to recite his infamous obedience lecture when Dustin's exclamation filled the room.

"Dad, look!" He pointed to the television. "It's her!"

Frank followed his son's gaze then stared in disbelief. There on his twenty-seven-inch color screen was the woman who'd occupied his thoughts for the better part of a month.

"Dad, it's Cadi."

"So I see." He was amazed Dustin remembered her name. "Quiet down so I can hear what's going on."

But it was too late. The interview with her had ended.

"And there you have it," the female reporter said. "Flooding and a tornado have devastated much of Cass County. But as you just heard, it's volunteers like these from Disaster Busters who can really make a difference in victims' lives, helping them literally find shelter in the time of storm."

"Dad, a tornado!"

"I heard, son, but the twister touched down days ago." Frank had been well aware of the flooding in that part of the state, too. "No more bad storms are in the forecast. I suspect Cadi's just helping with the cleanup."

"I hope she doesn't get hurt."

Frank glimpsed his son's fretful expression. He smiled. "She looks none the worse for wear to me—and that's after her car accident."

"Cadi was in a car accident?" A worried little frown creased Emmie's forehead.

"Yes, but she's all right. You just saw it for yourself." He clapped his hands together. "Okay. Enough TV. It's bedtime."

Frank headed for the stairs, leading the kids up toward their bedrooms. Emmie slipped in beside him and took his hand.

"Daddy, I'm scared."

He looked at his daughter. "Of what?"

"Of bad things like on TV."

"You're perfectly safe." He wanted to promise to protect her always, but hadn't he made that same vow to Yolanda and failed to keep it?

"Just trust in the Lord," Dustin spouted.

The reply seemed almost effortless and served as a rebuke to Frank.

" 'Trust in the Lord with all your heart and lean not on your own understanding,' Proverbs 3:5," Dustin recited proudly.

"That's Bible truth," Frank said. "Do you feel better now, Emmie?"

She bobbed her head. "Daddy, do you still like Cadi?"

"Sure." He hoped he sounded nonchalant. "But how do you know I even liked her in the first place?"

"I don't know," came the impish, singsong reply.

"It's 'cuz you get a funny look on your face sometimes," Dustin amended. "And once you left the computer on and I saw her picture."

Frank winced. He usually took precautions to safeguard his kids from the Internet. "I'll be more careful in the future."

They reached the top of the steps.

"Is she still mad at you like that day after church?"

"No, son, that's all taken care of now."

"Are you friends?"

"I suppose so."

"How come you don't ask Cadi on a date?"

"Maybe I will, Dustin. What do you think about that?" Frank chuckled at his son's surprised expression. But in the next moment, he saw this as an opportune time to find out his kids' opinions on the subject of his possibly dating Cadi. "Maybe I'll ask her out to dinner or something."

"Goodie. Can we come, too?" Emmie asked. "I've never been on a date before."

"And you won't be for another twenty years if I have my way." Frank laughed and swung the pixie into his arms.

She squealed with delight.

"Hey, Dad, how 'bout if we ask Cadi to our church's Fourth of July picnic?"

"We?"

"Yeah. She can be on our softball team."

"Aha, the true motive comes to light." Frank chuckled and deposited his daughter on her bed. "We'll see, okay?"

After tucking Emmie under her covers and giving her a kiss good night, Frank walked Dustin into his room.

"Think you'd kiss Cadi good night, Dad? She's pretty."

Frank put his hands on his hips and watched his son crawl in between the bedsheets. "How old are you?"

"Eight." Dustin rolled his eyes. "You know how old I am."

"Right. And I know you're too young to think about kissing girls, so keep your mind on sports, got it?"

"Got it." Dustin grinned.

Frank placed a kiss on his forehead and turned out the light. He rubbed his whiskered jaw as he made his way back downstairs. It encouraged him to hear his kids weren't averse to his asking Cadi out.

Perhaps it was time to take his relationship with her one step forward.

twelve

Cadi stared at the note Aunt Lou had left: "*Call Deputy Parker at your earliest convenience. No hurry.*"

Aunt Lou had also penned his phone number along with the date and time the message had been taken.

"Frank called?" Anticipation plumed inside of her.

"Yes, he did." Aunt Lou peeked around Cadi's shoulder. "It didn't sound like business."

"Cool." She pocketed the message. "I'll call him back."

"Call him now if you'd like. I have wash to do."

"I'll call him later, after I unpack."

A wry little smile played across Aunt Lou's face. "Officer Parker said he saw you on television."

"He did?" Cadi hoped that wasn't the only reason for his call. She'd been praying about getting to know Frank better, but she wanted the Lord to do the work in his heart. She figured she'd know that was happening if Frank initiated the relationship. The last thing Cadi wanted was to force something that wasn't God's will—as she had with Darrell.

"I must say, I'm very proud of you and your organization."

Cadi hugged her aunt. "Thanks for your prayers and encouragement. What would I ever do without you and your prayer chain?"

Releasing Aunt Lou, she lifted her duffel bag and lugged it upstairs where she began to unpack.

Aunt Lou followed her into her bedroom.

"I heard on the news that no one was killed or injured by the tornado," the older woman said, smoothing the skirt of her printed housedress. "That's good news."

"Actually, there was one injury, but the guy is going to be all right. He broke his arm getting his dog out of the house when the flooding began." Cadi managed a smile for her aunt, but the truth was floodwaters frightened her to the point of sheer panic.

"I trust the dog is all right, too."

Cadi nodded.

"Well, thank heaven for that." She collected Cadi's dirty clothes.

"Oh, Aunt Lou, don't pick up after me. I can throw my own clothes into the washing machine."

"You hush. I'm glad to do it." Aunt Lou headed for the doorway. "What would you like for supper tonight?"

"Anything's fine."

"Then it's cold chicken and potato salad."

"Yum." Cadi's stomach rumbled with anticipation, and she realized she hadn't eaten much all day.

"Oh, and. . ." Her aunt paused, and a huge smile spread across her face. "The car is going to be delivered tomorrow morning. I'm so excited."

"Hooray!" Cadi raised her hands and cheered. "You deserve it, Aunt Lou."

"Well, I don't know about that." An apple-red hue filled her cheeks. "But I'm very grateful for your generosity."

Cadi didn't feel she was particularly giving. Her aunt had, after all, taken her in as a child and brought her up to the best of her abilities. She'd nurtured Cadi's walk with the Lord and sacrificed through the years, showing true Christlike love. Now Aunt Lou's old clunker could barely chug its way to the grocery store and back. Cadi figured buying her a new car with the settlement she'd been awarded by Ross's car insurance company was only due reward.

"I never had a new car before. Never." Aunt Lou shifted the clothes in her arms. "And, of course, you can borrow it any time."

Cadi chuckled. "Thanks, but so far God has kept my van running, and now that it's paid off, thanks to the insurance money I received, I have one less financial burden."

Aunt Lou clucked her tongue and wagged her head. "Imagine Ross Hinshaw hiring an attorney because he thought you'd sue him. You're not that kind of a person—even though there was pain and suffering on your part and the accident was due to Ross's negligence."

"Yes, I suppose it is fair that I received some recompense." Ross's attorney had contacted her with the offer, hoping to stem future claims and possible losses, and a lawyer at church who specializes in family law helped seal the deal. "I'm just glad my medical bills were paid for."

"And then some! But Lonnie Mae said you could have gotten a lot more had you pressed the issue."

"Aunt Lou, we've discussed this before, and—"

"I know. I know. You're too good-hearted." Her aunt grinned affectionately. "To think you'd spend your money on an old goat like me. Lonnie Mae and the entire prayer chain couldn't believe it. A new car! For me!"

Cadi arched a brow. "I thought you were supposed to be praying on that prayer chain."

"We do pray, you sassy thing. But every so often we have to update each other on all the miracles that God has done."

Cadi replied with a grin. She didn't have anything against the prayer chain, but she certainly enjoyed teasing her great-aunt.

"Well, I'm off to the laundry room," Aunt Lou announced. "Come down to the kitchen when you're ready to eat. Everything is already prepared."

When her aunt left for the lower level, Cadi extracted Frank's message from her pocket then dug through her purse until she found her cell phone. She said a quick prayer for wisdom and calm for her sudden nerves then pressed his number into her keypad. She half expected to get a recorded message.

"Yep, Frank Parker here."

"Frank? It's Cadi. I'm returning your call."

"Well, hi—hang on a second."

She heard muffled voices before he returned.

"I sent my kids outside to play."

"You're home? I thought maybe I called your office."

"Cell phone."

"Ah." She sat down on the edge of her bed and folded one leg beneath her. "How've you been?"

"Good. What about you? How are you feeling?"

"Just great, actually."

"Glad to hear it. You were pretty banged up."

"I'll say."

That night was still pretty much a blur for Cadi; however, she and Frank had discussed it a couple of days later when she called to thank him for the beautiful bouquet of sunflowers, mums, daisies, and phlox. Two huge balloons and a box of chocolates had accompanied the arrangement. Aunt Lou took one look at the gifts and remarked that Frank certainly knew how to get a woman's attention.

"Cadi, do you have plans on Saturday night?"

The question shook her. "Saturday?"

"If you're available, I'd like to take you to dinner."

She couldn't contain her smile. "Why, Officer Parker, are you asking me on a date?"

"Oh, man. . .you're going to make me squirm, aren't you?"

Cadi laughed.

"Are you free or not?"

She decided he was rather fun to tease, but she chose not to push it. A date with Frank was what she'd been hoping and praying for!

"Dinner sounds nice. Thanks for the invite."

"I'll pick you up about six."

"I'll be ready."

When their call ended, Cadi stared at her cell phone, replaying their conversation in her mind. She couldn't wait to call Meg and tell her.

Then she flopped back on her bed and smiled. *And just wait until Aunt Lou and her prayer chain hear about this!*

thirteen

Cadi heard car doors slam and rushed to peek out her bedroom window. She glimpsed Frank emerging from his SUV followed by his two children.

He brought his kids? Frank never mentioned bringing his kids!

Cadi wondered if maybe he planned to drop them off at a babysitter's house. In the next moment, she noticed Frank's casual attire and knew at once that she'd overdressed for the occasion.

She hastened into the hallway and called downstairs to her aunt. "I'll be down in a minute!" Then she flung off the black dress and kicked off the heels. She grabbed a flattering khaki skirt out of the closet and pulled a teal sleeveless shirt over her head. Next she slipped her feet into brown sandals and grabbed her trim leather purse.

Finally she began to make her way down the steps, trying not to sound winded as her guests came into view.

Frank's daughter met her at the foot of the wide stairwell. "We came to take you on a date."

Cadi veiled her disappointment. She had envisioned a quiet, romantic evening alone with Frank.

"I never been on a date before," the girl added.

As she stared into the upturned, cherubic face, Cadi's regret vanished. The girl was baby-doll adorable. How could she resist?

Very simply, she couldn't.

"And I brung you these." Enthusiasm shone from her golden-brown eyes as she held out a bouquet of colorful but wilting flowers. "I picked 'em in my gramma's garden. My daddy said it was okay."

"How sweet. Thank you."

Making her way down the rest of the steps, Cadi accepted the flowers and gave the little tyke a hug. Aunt Lou was ready with a small vase and quickly placed the blooms in water.

"Thank you for asking me on your. . .date."

Cadi glanced at Frank and noticed his obvious chagrin.

"You remember my daughter, Emily, don't you?"

"Of course."

"And my son, Dustin."

Cadi smiled at the boy. "Hi, Dustin."

"I've never been on a date, either," he said, appearing embarrassed. "We're taking you out for pizza and then renting some movies. We can watch them together at our house."

"Sounds like—like a fun time." Cadi forced the upbeat inflection into her voice, unsure if the evening would be as eventful as she imagined.

She glanced at her aunt. "You've all met my aunt, Lou."

Everyone nodded, and her aunt sent her a curious look before seeing them to the door and walking them outside.

The humidity hung in the air like a thick drape, and Cadi felt beads of perspiration forming on her brow. As they ambled down the cement walkway, graced by multicolored petunias on either side, Frank nodded to the slate, four-door sedan parked in the driveway. The sticker was still on the rear window.

"New car?"

"Yes. Cadi purchased it for me," Aunt Lou replied. "Isn't she a beauty?" The excitement in her voice was unmistakable. "And she drives like a dream."

Cadi couldn't help smiling at the gleaming sedan. She felt pleased that she'd been able to purchase the car for her aunt. "She deserves it after all she's done for me."

"Nonsense." Aunt Lou bent over and plucked a weed from the flower bed. "You all have a good time now."

"We will," Dustin replied.

He and Emily raced to the curb.

Reaching his SUV, Frank opened the door for Cadi then

helped his children into the backseat and saw to it that they were buckled in.

"Why are cars always referred to as 'she'?" Cadi asked when Frank climbed behind the wheel. She fastened her seat belt and then gave her aunt one last wave.

"Motor vehicles, like women, are unpredictable," he retorted, "especially in bad weather."

Cadi glanced over her shoulder at Emily. "Did you hear what your dad said? He said we women are 'unpredictable.'"

A little frown creased Emily's brow. "What does that mean?"

Frank chuckled and started the engine.

"It means wishy-washy, like you never know what they're going to do next," Cadi said and aimed a look at Frank. "But I can think of a few men who are unpredictable, too."

"Me, too," Emily said with a weary-sounding sigh. "My grampa is unaddictable. First he wants to play checkers with Dustin, but he really promised to take me to the park."

"The voice of experience," Frank muttered with a grin. "All four, almost five, years of her life."

Cadi laughed and decided that at least this evening would be entertaining.

❧

Sitting in the armchair with his feet up on the ottoman, Frank couldn't shake the embarrassment numbing his body. He'd never seen his children behave in such an obnoxious manner, the little show-offs.

At the pizzeria, they shouted over each other, trying to impress Cadi with their many talents and attributes. Then they argued over movies at the rental store, attempting to drag Cadi into the middle of it. Once they'd arrived home, the two fought over who got to sit next to Cadi on the couch, and Dustin actually plopped his pillow in her lap and lay his head down, stretching out on the rest of the piece of furniture. This sent Emmie into a hissy fit until Cadi assured them both that she had plenty of lap for both kids.

So now there they were, Dustin reclined and Emmie curled up on Cadi while Frank sat in the adjacent leather chair. He'd be lucky if she ever spoke to him again.

"Oh, wasn't that a touching story?" Cadi said when Emmie's movie ended. "The princess shared her riches with her kingdom."

Emmie regarded her with wide eyes, looked back at the TV, and then at Cadi once more.

"It's a blessing to share the things God gives us, isn't it?" Cadi remarked.

Frank watched his daughter nod, and he had to admit feeling somewhat impressed that Cadi found a way to emphasize a moral in the story that hadn't been an obvious theme. In fact, Frank had seen this flick about five times, and he hadn't picked up on the giving aspect.

"Now we watch my movie," Dustin said, getting up and changing the DVD.

Emmie inched her pillow forward, and Frank could see fireworks coming.

"Emily Marie—"

Before Frank could say more, Dustin returned to the sofa. "Hey, move over!" He shoved his pillow into Emmie's.

"That'll be enough." Frank stood and clenched his jaw. His beautiful children had morphed into unrecognizable little brats. "Any more bad behavior and you'll go to bed without a second movie."

Dustin clamped his mouth shut, and Emmie didn't make a peep.

Well, maybe it's good that Cadi finds out right away what my life is like with two kids, Frank thought. *Now she won't have lofty expectations.*

He looked back at her and his children. They vied for her attention and, sitting together, they made a cozy sight that sent an odd sense of longing zinging through him. Still, he hoped Cadi didn't feel too imposed upon.

Standing to his feet, Frank realized he needed to be more

of a host. He caught Cadi's eye and smiled. "Can I get you a soda or something?"

"No, thanks."

"I'll take a soda," Dustin said. "How 'bout some popcorn?"

"Yeah. . ." Emmie perked up.

"No soda or popcorn for you two." Frank lowered himself back into his chair. "It's too close to bedtime. Besides, I was asking our *guest*."

The kids groaned in disappointment, and Frank shook his head at them.

They continued to watch the movie. Before long, Emmie fell asleep, and Frank took her upstairs to bed. When he returned, he took a seat on the couch on the other side of Cadi. He listened as Dustin talked her ear off about how he could ride his bike faster than the neighbor kid. Frank thought it was gracious of Cadi to act so impressed.

Stretching his arm across the back of the sofa, his gaze met hers, and he offered an apologetic look. Then he glanced at his son once again. "If you're not interested in this movie— that you picked out, I might add—we can turn it off and you can go to bed."

"Okay, okay." The boy took the hint, although his silence didn't last long. "Hey, Cadi, know what you smell like?"

"Dustin!" Frank could only imagine the forthcoming comparison, not that his son would intentionally insult Cadi.

She pulled her chin back. "I hope I don't smell bad."

"Uh-uh." Dustin grinned. "You smell real good. Like cake."

"Thanks." She smiled.

Relief poured over Frank, and he had to admit his son was right. He had been reveling in the sweet scent Cadi wore from the moment he sat beside her.

"Actually, you do smell good," he conceded, deciding to make light of Dustin's remark.

"I thought you'd never notice," she quipped.

"Haven't had the opportunity."

Their gazes met again, and they shared a laugh.

Suddenly Frank's mood lifted. The entire room seemed brighter.

❧

Cadi watched Frank trail his son up the steps. When his bedtime came, Dustin had protested, but his dad overruled, and now the boy all but stomped his way to the second floor.

She couldn't help smiling. Typical kid. She knew that from babysitting throughout her high school years and doing her share of nursery duty at church. Folks always said she had a special, God-gifted way with children; they took to her immediately, and judging from the way Dustin and Emily behaved tonight, she hadn't lost her touch.

Still wearing a grin, she stood and stretched as she glanced around the living room. Not for the first time, she became aware of the sparse décor in Frank's home. Even with a few odds and ends here and there, and several framed pictures on the oak entertainment center, the home had an impersonal feel to it. Cadi was hardly an expert on interior design; however, Aunt Lou tinkered and toyed with her decorating all the time and almost every corner of the old home had been filled with unique charm and loving touches.

Cadi's gaze lingered on the framed photos. Stepping forward, she paused to inspect the family shot. She picked it up and studied it. What impressed her most was Frank's demeanor. Gone were the hard angles and planes in his face. His features were softer in the picture. Beside him, a slim, auburn-haired beauty cradled a baby in her arms, and Cadi guessed the infant was Emily. Dustin looked no more than four or five, and he stood on the other side of his mother's wicker chair.

Cadi's gaze kept returning to Frank's smiling face. His dark eyes held sparks of happiness in their depths. In short, he looked altogether like a different man.

Hearing him clear his throat, she lifted her gaze.

Frank stepped toward her. "Thanks for being a good sport tonight. When my kids learned that I'd asked you out, they both begged and pleaded to come along. I gave in against my better judgment, and I'll admit it probably wasn't the smartest thing to take two rambunctious children with me on a first date." He shrugged his broad shoulders. "Then I figured you might as well see me—us—just as we are."

"I'll admit to feeling confused at first and maybe even a bit disappointed." Cadi smiled and shook her head. "But I think everything turned out fine. I love kids, and you should be proud of yours. Emmie's a sweet girl and Dustin is a nice, very thoughtful boy."

"I don't know how 'sweet' and 'nice' they were tonight." Frank moved closer and peered at the picture that Cadi still held in her hand.

"I hope you don't mind my looking at your photographs."

Frank wagged his head. "I don't mind."

"Is this your wife?"

"Was," he both corrected and confirmed. "She's been dead for over three years."

"I'm sorry to hear that." Cadi regarded the photo again. "She's beautiful. What was her name?"

"Yolanda." A rueful smile played across his lips. "She was the model domestic engineer. We owned a house outside of town, had a few acres of land, and Landi always had some project going on, whether she was planting flowers or wallpapering a bedroom. And she sure knew how to cook."

"I'm quite the opposite." Cadi set the picture back into place. "Maybe *hopeless* is the word to describe my domestic abilities. I've tried to cook and failed. My aunt attempted to instruct me, I've watched culinary shows on TV, and still it seems that every time I even go near the stove the smoke alarm goes off."

Frank's smile grew. "Well, if it's any consolation, the way to this man's heart isn't necessarily through his stomach." He chuckled. "Can I get you something to drink? Cola? A diet drink?"

"Um, sure."

Cadi was still trying to figure out what the way-to-this-man's-heart comment meant. But then she recalled their conversation at the zoo. His well-intentioned friends had set him up with women who cooked and baked.

Amused, she followed him into the kitchen. The decor was functional but unimaginative, like the living room.

"What'll it be?" Frank extracted a clear plastic bottle. "How 'bout a raspberry-flavored carbonated water?"

"Good enough." She took the proffered drink then eyed Frank. For some odd reason she couldn't imagine him taking a swig of this particular beverage.

He selected a diet cola for himself. Then, as if divining her thoughts, he said, "My kids' grandparents live next door, and when Lois, Yolanda's mother, found out that we were having a guest over, she straightened up and stocked the fridge."

"Nice gesture on her part."

"I'll say. I'm grateful to her." A sheepish grin accompanied Frank's reply. "I didn't think about cleaning the house."

Smiling, they reentered the living room.

"I suppose you're going to tell me that it's evident I need a wife."

Cadi took a seat on the couch, and Frank lowered his sizable frame beside her.

"Well, if cleaning and shopping is why you need a wife," she said, "I'm no candidate for the position." She saw no point in pretense. "And I already told you that I can't cook."

She sipped her carbonated water and watched Frank chuckle. Relaxing, he sat back, crossed his legs, and stretched his arm around Cadi's shoulders. She liked feeling his warmth and his strength, and she couldn't help but snuggle into him just a little.

"I must admit I find you both delightful and refreshing, not to mention pretty—and, as Dustin said, you smell good, too."

"Thanks." Cadi felt a blush creep up her neck and into her cheeks. "So, tell me about you."

A surprised look crossed his face. "Me? You already know about me."

"No, I don't. I know very little about you, really."

Frank took a gulp of diet soda. "What is it you want to know?"

"Well. . ." She paused in thought. "What's your favorite color?"

"Favorite color?"

A half smile curled his full lips. He looked deep into her eyes, causing Cadi to blush. "Blue. How's that?"

She felt flattered. "What do you do for fun?"

"What do you have in mind?"

"I'm not suggesting, Sergeant Parker." She arched a brow. "I'm *asking*."

"Oh."

Cadi flicked a glance upward. When she looked back at him, she noted his mischievous grin.

"Do you like football? Baseball? Hockey? Snowmobiling? Skiing?"

"Do you like those things?"

"Uh-huh." She nodded. "Number one Hawkeye fan."

He replied with a rumble of laughter before adding, "No shopping at the mall all day for you, eh?"

"Well, I do shop occasionally," she admitted. "But I'm hardly a mall rat."

Frank's grin was contagious.

"I don't ski, though."

"Ah. Well, neither do I. And the fact is I don't have much of a life apart from my kids and working."

"I may be able to help if you'd like to change that."

"Oh?" He appeared thoroughly amused.

"Sure." She couldn't pass up another chance to tease him. "Next time my friends and I plan to go somewhere fun, we could probably find it in our ever-so-gracious hearts to ask you along."

"Hmm."

Cadi watched the smile work on his lips as he fought it off. She, on the other hand, didn't even try to hide her grin.

At last he gave in and chuckled. Then he took another drink of his cola. "I read your blog," he said, changing the subject.

The statement surprised Cadi. "You did?"

He nodded. "I found it interesting." He paused. "I think the work you're doing to draw attention to the devastating effects of drunk driving is commendable. If the sheriff's department can be of any help, let us know."

"I will. Thanks, but. . ." She regarded him askance. "We're talking about you, remember?"

"Cadi, there's nothing to say about me." He balanced his soda can on his knee and stared at it.

She mulled it over. "Mind if I ask how your wife died?"

"No, I don't mind." He took hold of his soda can again, sat forward, and swung his gaze to hers. "Remember the tornado that ripped through this part of the state a few years back? It almost completely wiped out Rogan's Hill, a subdivision not far from here."

Cadi remembered. "That was a horrendous storm."

Frank agreed. "Yolanda was home with the kids when it hit. She did everything right. She grabbed the kids—Dustin was about five at the time and Emmie was only an infant—and took refuge in the basement. But when the house was destroyed, Landi. . ." He swallowed hard. "Well, she was killed. Neighbors found the kids crying, and Dustin was confused, but otherwise they were both unharmed." He paused. "Before the twister hit, Landi begged me to come home. She said she was frightened, but I—I told her she'd be okay. I felt I was needed on the job, not at home. I regret my decision to this day."

Although he spoke in a matter-of-fact way, Cadi saw the remorse in his eyes. She recognized the pain and guilt pooling in their depths. She knew it well.

"I'm so sorry."

"Me, too." He forced a smile. "But life goes on for those of us left behind, even when we might feel dead inside."

"I can relate all too well," she said emphatically. She shifted so she could see him better. "I wondered for years and years why I survived and my family didn't. I felt guilty for being alive."

His gaze met hers, and he appeared to be digesting everything she said. Then he reached out and touched her cheek.

They stared at each other for a long moment, and then Frank leaned forward and placed a light kiss on her lips. Cadi allowed her eyes to flutter closed, relishing the moment.

"Frank?"

Cadi started, hearing another female's voice followed by the thud of a closing door. She drew back and stared at Frank with wide eyes.

"My mother-in-law." He grinned. "She promised to sit with the kids."

"Oh." Cadi blinked.

Frank chuckled at what had to be her bewildered expression. "You didn't think I'd let you hitchhike home, did you?"

fourteen

Frank made the introductions, and Cadi smiled. "Pleased to meet you."

"Likewise." The bone-thin woman with short blond hair flicked a glance at her before looking back at Frank. "Are you ready to drive her home now, or do you want me to come back later? But not too much later. Church tomorrow, you know?"

Cadi sensed an immediate dislike coming from Lois Chayton and felt both puzzled and troubled by it. Did the woman resent her presence and think she'd come to take her daughter's place?

"We can go now." Frank's gaze shifted to Cadi. "Ready?"

"Sure."

It seemed an abrupt ending to an already peculiar first date. But as Cadi plucked her purse off the oak coffee table and made her way to the front door, she sensed Frank's former mother-in-law disapproved of her. She must have seen them kiss and drawn the wrong conclusions.

Frank opened the door of his SUV for Cadi, and she got in. He walked around and climbed behind the wheel.

"I don't think Lois likes me." She pulled the seat belt across her chest.

"It's nothing personal. That's just Lois. It takes her awhile to warm up to people." He started the engine then pulled away from the curb. "I should add that I, um, don't do a lot of dating."

"Hmm. Well, for what it's worth, I don't date a lot, either."

"I figured."

Curious, Cadi peered over at him.

"Will made a comment about you being ninety-five before having a gentleman friend."

"He said—what?"

Frank chuckled. "At the bank, the morning you were helping Mrs. Binder fill out the insurance form. . .well, she mentioned her 'gentleman friend' would pick her up. That's when Will made the comparison."

Cadi told herself she shouldn't be surprised by the antics of her wisecracking friend. "Oooh, just wait until I get my hands on him!"

Frank's hearty laugh made her smile, and the rest of the drive back to Waterloo passed with more quips and chuckles. Quite pleasant, given that most of the time Cadi regarded it as a tedious ride across the county at night.

All too soon, Frank slowed and parked his SUV in front of Cadi's house.

"On a serious note," he began, turning in his seat to face her, "I'd like to apologize once more for thinking the worst of your intentions when we first met."

"I accept this apology just like I did the last one." She tried to make out his expression in the darkness.

"Thanks." He killed the engine.

"I had a lot of time to think when I was recovering from the car accident," she added, "and it did cross my mind that in your line of work you almost have to be suspicious of everyone to a point."

"I do. That's true."

Releasing his seat belt, he unlatched his door and got out of the vehicle. Cadi did the same. Only too late did she realize Frank had intended to open the door for her. She smiled to herself and made a mental note to allow him that bit of gallantry in the future.

They traipsed up the walk, swatting away mosquitoes. The humidity hadn't abated, and no breezes stirred the moist, heavy air.

"The truth is, apart from my displaced notions," he said, "I liked you from the start. I guess that's what makes my initial actions even more regrettable."

"I'll admit to having my feelings hurt, but. . ." Cadi shook off the recollection before it had time to seed. "Let's just forget it, all right?"

"Sounds good to me."

They reached the front door.

Cadi looked up at him. She could just barely make out his features under the dim porch light. She glimpsed an expression of gentleness on his face. Maybe even something else that she couldn't quite put a finger on. "I had a nice time tonight."

"I'm glad. A little embarrassed, but glad you had a good time." A moment passed, and then he took a step forward and, placing his hand behind her head, he drew her lips to his.

A thought winged its way across Cadi's mind: *He makes my knees weak and my heart sing.*

The kiss deepened and senses took flight. But a moment later, the heavy wooden door swung open.

"I thought I heard you."

Aunt Lou's voice jolted Cadi back to the here and how. She stepped back while a self-conscious smile worked its way across her face.

"Why don't you two come inside? The bugs'll eat you up alive out there."

"Thanks, but I need to be on my way." Frank caught Cadi's hand and gave it a squeeze. "I'll call you."

"Okay. Bye. And thanks again."

She watched him go and entered the house. She closed the door behind her then sagged against it, marveling at the effect Frank had on her senses.

"Have a nice time tonight?"

"Um, yeah." She smiled at her aunt who had her hair wrapped in pink curlers that matched her short-sleeved pastel housedress. One of her favorite shopping channels lit up the TV screen.

"You could have asked him in, hon. I was on my way to bed."

Cadi waved off her aunt's suggestion. "Frank left his kids with their grandmother, and she asked him to hurry back."

"I see. . .and how was the date?" Aunt Lou lifted the sleek, black remote and turned off the television. "I like Frank a whole lot more than I ever liked Darrell."

"Me, too." Cadi laughed at her own reply.

"There's a genuine sparkle in his eyes. I had no qualms about you going off with him tonight. I sensed he was trustworthy."

"I'd have to agree with that." Cadi kicked off her sandals and set them on the steps. "His kids are sweet, too."

"I guess I didn't realize he had children until tonight when they walked into the house."

Cadi relayed the entire story to her aunt. About halfway through, they both got comfy on the classic-styled caramel-colored sofa.

"Oh, mercy! She was killed during that awful tornado?" Aunt Lou shook her head, mulling over the matter. "That was an awful storm. Iowa gets its share of twisters, you know, but that one was a doozy."

"I remember." Cadi had been taking classes at the technical college. When the tornado warning came, all staff and students were required to take cover in the stairwells.

"I just realized, Cadi, it appears you and Frank share a common denominator. You both have suffered tragic losses."

"I saw that connection. I recognized the pain in his eyes."

"That man does have expressive eyes, doesn't he?"

Cadi nodded, stood, and padded across the tapestry-styled carpeting and into the kitchen where she took a bottle of spring water from the refrigerator. Reentering the living room, she sat back down on the couch and took a long drink.

"By comparison, Darrell's eyes struck me as being cold and calculated. They looked like hazel-colored glass. No depth to them, you know?"

Cadi stifled a yawn. "Were you watching those goofy movies on that women's channel again? The heroines are always victims. I can't stand it."

Aunt Lou neither admitted nor denied it, much to Cadi's

amusement. Instead, her aunt stood from the couch and stretched.

"Time for bed. Church in the morning."

"I'm just going to finish my water. Then I'll turn off the lights and lock up before I go upstairs."

"Very good." She bent to kiss Cadi's cheek. "Sweet dreams."

She hadn't a doubt about that. She smiled at her great-aunt. "G'night, Aunt Lou."

❧

"Did you kiss her, Dad?"

Frank's jaw tensed as he sat at the breakfast table with his kids. He was tempted to tell Dustin it was none of his business whether he kissed Cadi or not. But then he figured he might as well be honest about it.

"Did you, Dad?" Emily asked. Her spoon hung in midair, halfway between her cereal bowl and her mouth. "Did you kiss her?"

He looked from one to the other. "You two are really something." He couldn't help a grin. "Yeah, I kissed her, all right? And I liked it, too. What do you think about that?"

Dustin grinned, and Emmie giggled and wrinkled her nose. "Ewwww."

Frank shook his head at them.

"Did Cadi like kissing you?" Dustin asked eagerly.

Frank recalled her starry-eyed expression. "Yeah, I think she liked it just fine." He shook off the pleasant memory and narrowed his gaze at his son. Frank didn't know whether to be concerned over Dustin's recent preoccupation with kissing or not. Was it merely a boyhood curiosity? Should he address the issue, or would it pass on its own?

"Did you ask her to the picnic, Dad?"

"No. To tell you the truth, I kind of forgot about the picnic. I might have to work that day, anyhow."

The boy's expression fell. "But I thought we were all going— like a family."

The comment cut Frank. "Let me see what I can work out."

He sensed the picnic carried more importance to his son than he'd first thought. "And I'll call Cadi and invite her. But let's get one thing straight: The three of us *are* a family. If someday I remarry, that lady will just be added to the family that we already have."

"But we're not a real family," Dustin muttered into his cereal bowl.

Frank leaned closer to his son. "Excuse me?"

Dustin lifted his chin and looked Frank in the eye. "We're not a real family. My Sunday school teacher said so. She said a real family has a father *and a mother*."

Frank clenched his jaw. He knew Dustin's Sunday school teacher. Paige Dunner. She enjoyed barging into Frank's life whenever she could drum up an excuse. To this point, he'd politely tolerated the meals she brought over to the house and the goodies she baked up for the kids on their birthdays or Valentine's Day and at Christmastime. But Frank wasn't about to allow Paige to manipulate his son so she could get to him.

"You're done with that Sunday school class. Hear me?"

Dustin's eyes grew wide. "But, Dad—"

"No exceptions."

Frank glanced across the table and, glimpsing the startled expression on Emily's face, softened his tone.

"I'm not punishing you, Dustin. I'm trying to protect you. That's my duty as your father. So we'll stop Sunday school for a while and I'll speak with Miss Paige, but you can still go to church."

"Will you come with us, Daddy?" Emmie asked, a pleading light in her amber eyes.

Frank paused, thinking it over, then expelled an audible sigh. "Oh, I don't know." He felt a sort of dread when he thought of attending the small church.

"Does Cadi go to church?" Dustin asked, his mouth stuffed with toast.

"Don't talk with your mouth full, son; and, yes, she goes to church."

"We could go to Cadi's church today," Emmie suggested on the sweetest note Frank ever heard, "and then you can come with us."

"Yeah, Dad, you came with us the time when Cadi was at our church."

"What is this? A conspiracy?" Frank stood and took his dishes to the sink. His entire body felt tense. His children were working his last nerve. He felt close to losing his patience.

But as he rinsed out his coffee mug, it occurred to him that perhaps his kids were starving for his attention. He tried to spend quality time with them on his days off, but perhaps it hadn't been enough.

He forced himself to take a deep breath, relax, and think things over.

Church? Attend services at Cadi's church this morning? No one there would regard him as the unfortunate widower struggling to raise two very precocious kids. What's more, he wouldn't have to withstand piteous stares from folks who knew and loved Yolanda. And, if he visited Cadi's church today, he wouldn't have to put up with overzealous unattached females like Paige Dunner. Of course, being with Cadi again would be a boon. Then again, she might have other plans.

He swung around and looked at his children. They stared back at him with expectancy glimmering in their eyes.

"Okay, I'll call Cadi and find out some things about her church—like the name of it and where it's located."

He glanced at his watch and decided they could very possibly make a later service.

Regarding his kids once more, he added, "This is a last-minute thing, but maybe it'll work out."

They let out a happy whoop.

"But I'm not promising anything." Frank had to raise his voice above their victorious cheers to add, "So don't get your hopes up."

In reply Dustin and Emily peered into their cereal bowls and grinned.

fifteen

The wind shifted, bringing in a cooler breeze and a reprieve from the hot humid air. Cadi decided it was perfect weather for the first of July.

She drew in a deep breath as she stood outside the church's front entrance waiting for Frank and his children to arrive. She'd been surprised by his phone call at eight thirty this morning, during which he asked to visit her church. He didn't give a lengthy explanation, and Cadi felt puzzled. Was he just checking her out further, making sure she belonged to a church whose pastors preached the same biblical beliefs as Adam Dremond? Cadi had no worries there, although Riverview Bible Church was about ten times larger than Pastor Dremond's quaint little church in Wind Lake. Regardless of the reason, Cadi felt a swell of anticipation at seeing him again.

"Are you waiting for me?"

Hearing the familiar voice, Cadi suppressed a groan and glanced to her left. Darrell Barclay stood on the sidewalk, a few feet away, wearing an expensive suit and a lopsided grin. He'd never called to see if she was all right after the car accident, and even though she saw him here and there at church, they hadn't spoken to each other. Now Cadi wondered how he could have the nerve to approach her and be so arrogant—and so wrong.

"No, I'm not waiting for you, Darrell." She looked away.

He stepped forward. "I thought perhaps you wanted to apologize."

She arched a brow and regarded him again. "Apologize for what?"

"For humiliating me at my brother's birthday party, of

course." Another step closer and Cadi got a whiff of his temple-throbbing cologne. "What kind of girl are you to leave my parents' house with some *lowlife* like Ross Hinshaw?"

"I'm a girl who makes mistakes like everyone else," Cadi replied in her own defense.

In the next moment, she caught sight of Frank and his kids walking across the parking lot, heading for the entrance. She realized she already possessed stronger feelings for Frank—and amazingly felt closer to him—than Darrell.

"Our dating relationship was one of my biggest mistakes," she added with a quick glance in his direction. "Now if you'll excuse me, my visitors have arrived."

She marched off to meet the Parkers, slowing her strides as she neared. When the children saw her, they raced to meet her.

"Hi, you guys." She noted Dustin's striped, short-sleeved dress shirt and navy slacks and Emily's frilly yellow dress. "You both look so nice."

"So do you." Emily hugged her around the waist.

"Thanks." Cadi tousled Dustin's sandy-colored hair then turned to Frank, who was dressed in tan slacks and a blue Oxford shirt with a coordinating necktie. She was about to remark on his dapper appearance when she noticed the dark glance he flicked toward the entrance doors.

A quick peek over her shoulder, and Cadi saw Darrell disappear into the building.

"Everything all right?"

Cadi looked back at Frank and smiled. "It is now." She took Emily's hand and slipped her other arm around Dustin's shoulders. "Come on. Let's go inside. We don't want to be late."

They reached the glass-paned doors and entered, then strode through the bustling foyer and into the expansive sanctuary. People milled about as the pianist played a medley of up-tempo hymns.

"I saved some seats for us," she told Frank. "And I have a big surprise for you," she said to the kids. "You're invited to attend children's church today as two very special guests. You'll even get to pick a prize out of the guest box if you attend. But you don't have to go. It's up to you and your dad."

They found their places. Cadi picked up her Bible and notebook from one of the padded, dark green chairs and explained Riverview's children's program to Frank and the kids.

"What do you think, Dustin and Emily? Would you like to go to children's church today?"

Both kids turned to their dad for permission.

"You can go if you want," he said.

"We'll come and get you right after our service up here is over," Cadi promised. She looked at Frank, sitting to her right. "Afterward, my aunt insists you all come over for lunch."

"Can we, Dad?" Dustin's eyes sparked with eagerness.

"Yeah, can we?" Emily maneuvered her way onto Cadi's lap.

"We're sort of intruding on your day," Frank said with a note of contrition in his voice.

"Yes, you are—and I'm rather happy about it." She noticed his whole demeanor seemed to relax.

Next she watched him take in his surroundings. Cadi sensed that not much escaped his scrutiny. She felt suddenly very safe, even protected, in Frank's presence.

The service began with the choir singing a soul-stirring number. Then, while an appointed member of the congregation stood and read from the book of Luke, Meg and Aunt Lou filed into the row. Cadi, Frank, and the children moved down to accommodate them. After the choir sang again, Pastor Bryant dismissed the children. Moments later, Meg's younger sister, Beth, showed up to escort Dustin and Emily downstairs.

The kids appeared tentative at first, but Beth soon won them over, and they followed her out of the sanctuary.

The aisles filled up with children from ages four to twelve and, during the din of the exodus, Cadi leaned over to Frank and explained, "Meg's sister is one of the volunteers who helps with children's church."

He nodded in understanding, although Cadi sensed he had already figured out that much.

"Tell me something else," he said.

"Okay."

With another incline of his head, he indicated down the row of seats. "Do I have competition?"

A little frown tugged at her brows as Cadi peered around Frank's muscular frame. She spotted Darrell sitting at the end of the aisle, and annoyance filled her being.

She straightened. "No competition there. Believe me." While she didn't dare hope they'd be friends someday, she did wish that she and Darrell would eventually develop a mutual respect for each other. They were, after all, both Christians. But until Darrell got over himself, a platonic friendship seemed impossible.

At this point, Cadi merely wanted to put some distance between them. In fact, she had assumed that distance already existed. She couldn't imagine why Darrell decided to approach her this morning, unless it was to goad her. Except she didn't think he was speaking to her. He never called once to check on her recovery from the car accident and, with regard to that fateful night, she supposed she did owe Darrell some sort of apology. She'd made some wrong choices and paid the consequences. What's more, Cadi regretted her harsh words to Darrell earlier.

She opened her mouth to relay all this to Frank, but before she could utter another word, Pastor Conner began his sermon.

Cadi sat back and made a mental note to explain things to Frank later. In the meantime, she opened her Bible and tuned in to the preaching of God's Word.

❧

"I love you, Cadi."

The words hit Frank like a sock in the jaw. Next he watched his little daughter throw her arms around Cadi's waist and hug her good-bye. Dustin was quick to get in on the action, and Frank heard his son repeat Emily's phrase. "I love you."

Cadi laughed. "I love you guys, too." She helped them climb into the SUV while Frank stood by feeling dazed.

Kids don't know what they're saying, he rationalized. *They just met Cadi. They can't possibly love her.*

Except the same words had been on the tip of his tongue all afternoon.

He gave himself a firm mental shake. This relationship was moving way too fast.

"I'm glad you could come today." Cadi stood in front of him, her slender chin tipped upward, and she searched Frank's face. "I had fun."

"It was nice. Thanks for inviting us over after church. We didn't intend to stay so long."

The remark came out a bit more stilted than he intended. He watched as the smile slipped from Cadi's face.

"Anything wrong?"

"No." He wagged his head. "I just need to get the kids home."

"Oh, sure. I understand." She glanced into the SUV's open window and waved.

"Don't forget the Fourth of July picnic!" Dustin called.

"I won't."

Frank cleared his throat. "Cadi, about the picnic. . ."

She turned toward him. Her eyes were as blue as the sky and her smile as brilliant as an evening sunset. She wore an expression of both expectancy and hopefulness, and he hated to disappoint her.

"I might have to work," he muttered, averting his gaze.

"No big deal. Just let me know. Unless there's a disaster somewhere calling my name, I've got no plans yet for the Fourth."

Frank grinned in spite of himself. He threw a glance over his shoulder at the porch where Cadi's great-aunt, along with two neighbors who had stopped by, sat on white wicker furniture chatting. He wanted to kiss Cadi before he left, but not in front of an audience.

He settled for a quick hug and figured it was probably for

the best anyway. He had a feeling he needed to take a step back and examine this relationship with a cool head filled with common sense before moving full throttle ahead. So much had happened both last night and today that Frank felt like he'd lived an entire month in less than twenty-four hours.

"Thanks again for everything." He walked around his vehicle and climbed in behind the wheel. The kids shouted good-byes to Cadi as he pulled away from the curb.

As he drove the distance back to Wind Lake, Frank had plenty of time to reflect on everything that occurred from this morning until now. After a stirring but pride-splitting message from the pulpit, he had retrieved Dustin and Emily from children's church. The first question to leave their lips was, "Can we come back next week?"

Next, Cadi's great-aunt had served up one of the tastiest luncheons Frank had ever eaten. They watched a little football on television, and he chuckled to himself now, thinking how both Cadi and her aunt enjoyed the sport. Unconventional women—that they were. Refreshing, actually, as far as Frank was concerned. He found it amazing, too, that Dustin and Emmie took to Aunt Lou almost as fast as they'd taken to Cadi. They had two sets of grandparents who loved them and aunts and uncles and cousins—why did they think Cadi and her aunt were so special?

Frank kneaded his whiskery jaw and went back to his unconventional theory. He couldn't recollect ever seeing his mother, mother-in-law, or sisters watch sports on television—at least not voluntarily. Making it even more incredible that Cadi and her aunt enjoyed a good ball game was the fact that Iowa laid no claim to any major league teams. Today they cheered on the Green Bay Packers and Milwaukee Brewers. And then the truth emerged: Aunt Lou admitted having grown up in Wisconsin. Her bias had rubbed off on Cadi.

Frank grinned as nighttime fell down around his vehicle. A glance into the rearview mirror revealed that his children were dozing. They'd had an action-packed day.

And they're enamored with Cadi.

And so am I.

Now what do I do?

Frank had to admit to feeling wary, if not downright petrified. Cadi had captured his heart the day he met her. Was such a thing really possible? Could it be real? The last thing he wanted was to get hurt—and for his kids to get hurt. Things just seemed too perfect. There had to be a catch.

He thought over the conversation he had with Cadi this afternoon when they took the kids for a walk to the park. She said she'd babysat all through high school, almost every weekend, which, Frank concluded, explained her practiced way with children. He heard the story of Cadi's two years in foster care and how by God's divine guiding hand of grace, the state had located and contacted Aunt Lou who, of course, stepped up to claim her only heir. Cadi knew the heart-twisting, soul-searing pain of tragically losing a loved one. She related to the guilt that sometimes followed. She understood when he mentioned feeling dead inside for the last few years, and Frank saw the tiny tear that formed in the corner of her eye when he confessed that she made him feel alive again.

"I'm touched, Frank," she'd said as they sat on the park bench. "Thanks for telling me that."

But now he felt like an imbecile. He should have kept his mouth shut. He'd shown Cadi his weakest, most vulnerable side this weekend, a part of himself he hadn't revealed to anyone since Yolanda's death.

Not even to God.

Frank reached the townhouse he rented from his in-laws and parked his SUV. He got out then woke up his children and helped them from the vehicle. Once they were in the house, he helped the two wash up and get ready for bed. After tucking the kids in, he gathered their dirty clothes and carried them to the basement laundry room. He threw a load in the washer then trudged back upstairs. Returning to the living room, he heard a knock on the back door and answered it. His mother-in-law stood there wearing a fuzzy blue bathrobe.

"Can I come in? I'd like to talk with you."

"Sure." Frank let her in and closed the door.

"Kids in bed?"

"Yep."

"They were up awfully late tonight."

He knew Lois didn't mean anything by the remark, but it irritated him just the same. Stepping away from the door, he walked farther into the kitchen and leaned against the kitchen table.

"Is that why you came over? To reprimand me?"

"Of course not. I was just. . .well, concerned when I didn't hear from you or see the kids this morning." She paused and regarded him askance.

"We visited Cadi's church. I should have told you so you wouldn't have expected the kids. I apologize."

"You took Dustin and Emmie to another church this morning?" The dismay in her voice was evident. "What's that supposed to mean? Our church isn't good enough for you anymore?"

Frank shook his head. "Not the case."

"Let me remind you that it's the very church Yolanda grew up in. Dad and I still attend there. Your parents attend there, too, now. Our friends and—"

"And that's the problem," Frank cut in, fighting to keep the impatience out of his tone. "Whenever I step inside that church, I feel suffocated by the past and by everyone who loved Yolanda."

"When did you reach that conclusion? After you met Cadi?"

"Yes, although it's been coming for a while." Frank stared, unseeing, at the oak cupboards. "Adam Dremond brought up the subject months ago."

Lois folded her bony arms. "Have you been dating Cadi since she and her colleagues came to town to help with that gas explosion?"

"No, but that's when we met. We just started seeing each other." It galled him to give an account to his deceased wife's mother. On the other hand, he depended on Lois for so many things involving the kids and his home. To that degree he figured he owed her an explanation.

"I suppose if you marry this woman Dad and I will never see the children again."

"What?" Frank swung his gaze at her. Her remark seemed irrational. "What are you talking about? Marriage? I just started dating Cadi."

"Well, I suppose it's bound to happen sooner or later—your getting remarried, that is."

"Lois, if I should remarry, I promise never to stand in the way of your relationship with Dustin and Emmie. They love you very much. You're an important person in their lives." He shifted his stance. "Look, it's too soon for me to be confident in where my relationship with Cadi is going, but I do know I have to start living again. I think she's pretty, I admire her tenacity, and I enjoy the way she makes me feel when we're together."

"Hmm, sounds serious." Lois tipped her head. "I wonder what Yolanda would think."

"Landi would want me to be happy."

"What about Paige Dunner? I thought you liked her. She's pretty, too, and Yolanda thought the world of her." A faraway gleam entered Lois's hazel eyes. "She always said Paige would make an excellent wife and mother."

"I'm sure she will, but I'm not the guy who'd make her an excellent husband."

"What about Nicole Russell? She goes to our church. She's single. She and Yolanda went to high school together."

"I know who you're referring to, but there's no. . .no chemistry there with either of those women."

"Yes, well, I already saw a bit of that, um, chemistry you feel for Cadi."

"I kissed her. Big deal." Frank grew increasingly uncomfortable. His so-called "love life" was none of Lois's business, and he preferred to keep it that way. "Listen, it's late, and I need to get some shut-eye."

He walked around Lois and left the room. No more than a minute later, he heard her leave through the back door.

sixteen

Rain pelted the window of the Disaster Busters office then dribbled down the pane like so many teardrops.

Cadi released a blasé sigh and stared out over the almost empty parking lot. Puddles formed on the black asphalt. It had been gloomy and rainy for a good part of a week, and Cadi was beginning to feel a bit dreary herself. Her mood, she acknowledged, was not only due to the weather but the fact that she hadn't heard from Frank in over a week.

On the Fourth of July he'd called to say the picnic had been rained out, and he hadn't called again. Then, two days ago, she phoned him to ask if the kids wanted to attend children's church. Frank said he had to work and Dustin and Emily were spending the day with their grandparents. He ended their conversation soon after that, leaving Cadi no choice but to wonder if she'd offended him somehow. Either that or Frank was put off by what he had termed his "competition."

Cadi had meant to explain about both her run-in with Darrell as well as their nonexistent relationship on the day Frank and his kids came to the house for noon dinner, but she never got the opportunity. Even so, Sergeant Frank Parker didn't strike her as a guy who would be deterred that easily. It had to be something else.

Lord, You know his heart. You know all things. I don't have peace about calling Frank again. Is it best that he and I don't contact each other? Is this Your will? I'm hurt and disappointed, but I know that Your will and not mine is and always will be best.

She squared her shoulders, leaving the matter in the hands of her heavenly Father, and moved away from the window. She glanced at the clock on the walnut credenza. Four thirty.

She was tired and listless, and with the dismal skies outside, it felt like the time should be much later.

Her gaze shifted to the accumulating paperwork in need of filing, and Cadi decided to make a pot of coffee to infuse some artificial enthusiasm into her system. A short while later, with a mug of rich-smelling brew beside her on the scarred desktop, she began sorting the documents she'd allowed to pile up.

About an hour later, she was just finishing up when a knock sounded. Her office door stood ajar, and glancing in that direction, she saw Darrell standing in the threshold.

He walked in without waiting for her reply. "Some of us are going to the steak house for dinner. We decided to meet here. Want to come?"

"No, thanks." She was puzzled by the invitation.

"I can see you weren't expecting me."

"To say the least." Cadi closed the filing cabinet drawer and walked around the desk. Sitting on its corner, she folded her arms and regarded him askance. "What are you doing here?"

"Well. . ." He stepped toward her. "I decided I'm ready to hear whatever it is you have to say."

Oh, don't tempt me. She fought against the mounting cynicism.

"I'm ready to accept your apology." He stuffed his hands into the side pockets of his crisp navy slacks. "I wasn't ready before. Now I am."

"I'm so flattered, Your Highness." She bowed.

"Oh, quit the theatrics. I'm serious."

Cadi smiled at his retort.

"Did you ever think of how embarrassed I was the night of that party when you left with Ross Hinshaw of all people? You chose him over me?"

Her amusement vanished. "No, I guess I didn't consider your feelings—because you were rather preoccupied with a certain woman with long blond hair."

Darrell rolled his eyes. "So you left with Hinshaw because

you were jealous?" He nodded. "I suppose that makes more sense."

"I left with Ross because I was hurt," she corrected. "All I wanted to do was go home, and he offered me a ride. It was a bad choice on my part, even though I had no idea Ross was drunk."

"Hmm." Darrell strode to the desk and sat on its edge next to Cadi. She refused to encourage him and walked to the door.

"I admit my actions that night bordered on irrational," she said, "and I'm sorry for any embarrassment I caused you." There. She'd apologized.

"Apology accepted." He flashed a practiced grin, and Cadi wondered how she'd ever found him charming. "Now, how about dinner at the steak house?"

"I'm not hungry. Thanks." She set her hand on the doorknob, hoping Darrell would take the hint.

"Our friends say we look good together, Cadi."

"Our friends?" She couldn't imagine to whom he referred. "I don't believe we share the same friends."

He chuckled at the remark. "We're all brothers and sisters in Christ. Your friends are my friends and vice versa. It's just that my friends are climbing the social ladder and gaining respect—earning money."

Cadi thought about her closest friends—Meg, Will, Jeff, and Bailey. They climbed a different "ladder of success"—one of service to God and helping other human beings in their time of need. Of course, Christians in positions as bankers, lawyers, and corporate executives were needed, also, but Cadi couldn't imagine fitting into that social circle. She saw that fact clearly now.

"It's true that you've disappointed me on several occasions," Darrell said, "but I'm willing to give our relationship another chance. I've discussed the matter with several godly individuals here at church, and each of them persuaded me to cultivate, not terminate, our relationship."

She gaped at him, noting the one-sidedness of his logic. *God, help me here. Give me patience with this man.*

"What do you say, Cadi?"

She shook her head. "Darrell, seriously, our relationship was terminated months ago. I just didn't realize it then. But I do now."

He appeared taken aback. "Months ago?"

She softened. "We're all wrong for each other. Let's face it: You want and need someone different than who I am. You want a woman who is polished, sophisticated." She stopped herself before adding "arm ornament" to the list.

Darrell stuck out his lower lip and sort of shrugged in silent agreement. "You polish up rather nicely."

He meant it as a compliment, and to a certain extent she was flattered. But Cadi would never forget his wandering eyes at the party and the fact that he hadn't felt concerned enough about her even to make one quick phone call to check on her recovery after the accident. What's more, he considered Disaster Busters a waste of time and nothing more. And then there was his walk with the Lord to consider. In Cadi's opinion, it appeared perfect, almost superficial, although she didn't doubt that Darrell was a Christian.

"You have possibilities, Cadi."

"So do you." She smiled. "But we're not right for each other." She glanced down at her attire. "I wear a sweatshirt and blue jeans to work."

"Yes, but—"

"I'm an EMT, and you can't stand the sight of blood."

"A lot of couples have vastly different likes and dislikes—"

"Darrell, I'm in love with somebody else."

Cadi couldn't believe the statement had flown out of her mouth with so little effort.

Darrell, however, didn't appear too surprised. "The guy with the two kids? He was in church a couple of Sundays ago?"

"Yes." She was still reeling from her admission. Had she really said "love"? When did that happen? How could it have happened? Frank confused her most of the time. Love him? Impossible.

Then she recalled how she felt in his arms, all weak-kneed and her heart singing like a bird in the springtime. He shared a side of himself that made her feel special and needed. His children were well-adjusted despite losing their mother so tragically. They looked up to Frank, respected and adored him, and that alone told Cadi a lot about the man, even though when they talked that Sunday afternoon, he'd admitted to wrestling with his relationship with God.

Nevertheless, the fanciful workings of her heart dared to hope in love and a happily-ever-after with Frank.

"Must be divorced, huh?"

"Widowed." She blinked and gathered her wits. "Darrell, I think you need to leave. I—I've got some errands to run."

"What does he do for a living? Does he make more money than I do? I hope you're considering these important questions."

She ignored him and crossed the room. She saw no point in discussing Frank any further—especially with Darrell. Opening the bottom drawer of her wooden desk, she lifted out her purse.

"I should get going, and you don't want to miss your friends. The steak house gets really crowded."

Darrell glanced at his pricey gold wristwatch. "Yes, I suppose."

He sauntered to the door in a way that exuded self-confidence. She followed him out, turning off the lights before closing up the office behind her.

"Well, have fun tonight." She forced a polite inflection into her voice.

When Darrell didn't reply, she paused and regarded him with a curious frown. He just stood there, statue still and staring over her shoulder. What had seized his attention?

Oh, well, none of her concern.

She whirled around and took a forward stride, instantly colliding with none other than the elusive deputy himself, Frank Parker.

Frank had dropped in to see Cadi on a whim. Purely a whim. He'd had business at the courthouse, and the idea of her being a mere couple of miles away nearly drove him to distraction.

For the last nine days, she'd occupied his thoughts almost every hour, and when she didn't, Dustin or Emily served as a reminder each time one of them mentioned her name.

Very simply, he wanted to see her again. He *had* to see her again.

But when he entered the church and neared the Disaster Busters office, after asking directions, he was brought up short by what he first believed to be some sort of lovers' quarrel. He recognized Cadi's voice and felt pinned to the tile floor, unable to breathe, let alone move.

Then he heard what he could only describe as an answer to his deep-down, most personal prayers.

A sign. He had longed for a sign. Move forward or turn tail and run?

He now felt confident in taking the next few steps ahead.

And, as Cadi stood just inches away, having fallen right into his arms, he watched her face turn from pink to a very pretty crimson. Her eyes, on the other hand, held that proverbial deer-caught-in-the-headlights stare.

"You okay?" Frank steadied then released her. "I hope you didn't reinjure those ribs when we crashed just now."

"I—I'm fine," she stammered.

She looked flustered, and Frank resisted the urge to chuckle. Instead, he held out his right hand to Darrell and introduced himself. Under the circumstances, he had no qualms about being cordial to the guy.

The other man replied in a brisk but polite manner and quickly excused himself, saying he had a dinner engagement.

Frank stifled a guffaw and peered at Cadi.

"This isn't what you think," she said in a whispered tone. "Darrell stopped by to—well, you see, I did sort of owe him an apology, and—"

"Cadi, relax. I wasn't eavesdropping or anything, but I heard enough to know that there's nothing going on between you two, okay?"

"How much did you hear?" A mix of suspicion and dread swept over her features.

Frank was so encouraged he felt almost giddy. "I heard you tell him to leave."

"Oh." Cadi tried in vain to hide a grimace.

"I also heard you say something about running errands. I just got off duty. Do you have time to grab a bite to eat?"

Her blue eyes searched his face. "I was beginning to think you didn't want to see me again."

He noted her wounded expression and took hold of her hand. "Let's talk over supper. How 'bout it?"

seventeen

Cadi toyed with the handle of her stoneware coffee mug as she sat across the table from Frank. She watched him eat the last of his honey ham sandwich, complete with thick slices of cheese, lettuce, tomatoes, mustard, red onions, and cucumbers. It resembled the salad she'd eaten except it'd been stuffed between two fat pieces of whole wheat and herb bread.

She grinned as he polished off the last of his meal. A couple of weeks ago Aunt Lou had commented that Frank and his kids were fun to cook for because of their hearty appetites.

He pushed his plate to the end of the long, narrow table. "So, you see, I never wanted to hurt you," he said, wrapping up his explanation for not contacting her sooner. "I just thought maybe things between us were moving too fast."

She hid a wince and dared not ask if he still felt that way. She suspected he'd heard her blunder while speaking with Darrell earlier. Should she explain? Maybe she didn't mean "love"—if not, then what *did* she mean?

"I have to protect my kids," Frank continued. "They adore you, and I don't want them to get hurt. I don't want any of us to get hurt."

"Me, either." She did wonder, however, what point he was trying to make. Did he want to see her more? Less? Not at all?

She allowed her gaze to wander around the rustic coffee and sandwich shop, admiring its old-time Western decor. From her vantage point, she could see through the front windows, and she noticed it had begun to rain again.

"So what do you want to do about. . .things?" She looked back at Frank. He still wore his uniform—the tan shirt and green trousers. He'd mentioned that he knew his shift would end after his business at the courthouse was completed, so he'd driven his own vehicle from Wind Lake, but he hadn't found time to change clothes.

He rotated his broad shoulders in response to her question. "What's there to do?" He wiped his mouth with a white paper napkin then set it on the table. "Would you like some dessert?"

"Um, no. . ." Cadi felt so confused her head spun.

"I talked to Adam Dremond last week. He told me there are folks still struggling with housing issues as well as other basic needs while they wait for their insurance to cover their losses. He said in some cases it can take up to three months—or longer—to get a claim paid."

Cadi marveled at the lengthy time frame and figured it depended on the insurance company. Her allotment from the car accident had been issued immediately, it seemed.

"Anyway, donations are still coming in from the Web page. Adam is pleased."

"Excellent. I'm glad the site proved to be a helpful tool."

Their gazes met and, as always, Cadi felt like she could lose herself in Frank's deep brown eyes. Next she watched as a smile worked its way up his face.

He reached across the table and placed his palm over the top of her hand. "It's good to see you, Cadi. I'm glad I gave in to my impulse and dropped in on you."

"I'm glad you did, too."

They lingered at the table a few more minutes then pushed back their wooden chairs. Frank had already paid for the meals, so they strode out of the restaurant and ran through the downpour to his fawn-colored SUV.

Inside, they shook off the rain and buckled up; then Frank started the engine.

"Thanks for dinner."

"You're welcome, except you didn't eat much."

"I've got a lot on my mind."

"Nothing to do with your verbal exchange with—what's his name? Darrell?"

Cadi laughed. "No. I actually hadn't given him much thought at all." The truth was she'd been working up her nerve to ask Frank where she stood with him.

They rode in silence for several long minutes.

"You sure everything's okay?"

"Yep."

She watched the rain stream down the windshield as the wipers kept time with the instrumental light jazz playing on the radio. They drove through one puddle and then another.

"I hope the streets aren't affected by all this rain." She craned her neck, trying to view what lay ahead. This section of road had flooded in the past.

"Roads are fine, Cadi. I know them as well as my own reflection."

"Then I'll take your word for it." She forced herself to sit back and relax.

"We've had bad weather lately, but nothing like the other parts of the state."

"Don't I know it! Some places looked like war zones."

"That's what twisters can do." Frank grew pensive.

Regret filled Cadi. "I hope I didn't trigger painful memories for you."

"You didn't. It actually helps to talk to someone like you, someone objective, outside the family, and who can identify with my intense loss." She saw him flash a smile as they passed under a streetlight.

"I feel the same way."

"I can tell."

A little grin tugged at her mouth as she realized how bittersweet their connection was. A natural disaster.

"Well, I must admit that responding to the flood situation in Cass County was frightening for me, but Disaster Busters was in charge of finding folks temporary lodging. Had I been part of the rescue efforts, I might have had serious issues."

"Did you ever learn to swim?"

"Sure, but in chlorinated pools. You and I both know the

best swimmers can be rendered defenseless in floodwaters."

"True enough."

"The currents alone can be deadly."

"Agreed."

"Swimming in pools, I can handle." She repositioned herself in the leather seat. "But floods. . ." She didn't finish her sentence, distracted once more by the weather outside. "I just wish it would stop raining."

"Cadi, don't worry. We're safe," he said as if reading her troubled thoughts. "I'd know it if we weren't. There aren't any flash flood warnings in effect around here, and I'm familiar with the highways, even the side roads, prone to flooding in this county. This isn't one of them."

She considered his words and felt somewhat reassured.

She settled back in her seat and took a deep breath. "Thanks. I feel better."

"Good." There was a smile in his voice. "Tell you what, I'll drive you home now, and your aunt can take you over to church tomorrow to pick up your van. I'm sure it'll be safe enough in the parking lot overnight."

Cadi shook her head. "I'm a big girl. I shouldn't have burdened you with my childish insecurities."

"Listen, we all have them, childish or not. Let me help you out. It's no trouble."

His offer put her at ease all the more. "Really? You'd do that for me?"

"Of course I would." He stretched his arm across the distance between the seats and took her hand. "I'd consider it an honor."

How gallant, Cadi thought. Suddenly her thoughts about the rain dissipated.

Frank drove the rest of the distance to her home. He parked and they exited the vehicle then ran through the rain and up onto the front porch.

She faced him. "Can I ask you something? I mean—I just want to make certain I heard you correctly at the coffeehouse."

"Sure." He leaned against one of the round, vertical posts that adjoined the spindled railing.

"What I think I heard you say," she began again, trying to be as diplomatic as possible, "is that our relationship is moving too fast and that you want to back off."

"That was my mind-set initially." He chuckled, perhaps at himself. "But the truth is I don't want to back off. I'd like to see you every day if I could."

She smiled, feeling encouraged. "That would be fine with me. But am I to understand that you don't want me to see Dustin or Emily because you're afraid they'll get hurt?"

He looked down at his boots before returning his gaze to hers. "It's almost too late for that, and it's my fault. The reality is my kids will be hurt if they *don't* get to see you."

"I'll be a little hurt, too, but you're their father, and I will, of course, abide by whatever you decide."

Frank regarded her in a kind of thoughtful awe. "You'd really be hurt? You're that fond of my kids?"

"Of course I am." She laughed. "I mean, they really feed my self-esteem because they think I'm so wonderful. How could I not adore them right back?"

Frank chuckled. "You've got a point there."

"All kidding aside, you've got a couple of wonderful, thoughtful, sensitive children, and that says a lot about you as their parent."

"I can't take all the credit. I get a lot of help."

"I don't think you give yourself enough credit."

He shrugged, and a faraway look entered his eyes as he stared off somewhere over her head. "I feel like I've been living life on autopilot until now."

"And God knew it, and He protected you by enabling you to raise your kids and maintain your job."

Frank's gaze returned to Cadi, and she glimpsed the intensity in his eyes. "And now God brought you into my life."

Cadi felt like cheering. Frank was coming back to life in more ways than one. His spiritual life seemed to be returning, too.

Taking a step toward him, she stood on tiptoe and kissed his rough jaw. His arms enveloped her, and in that moment, she knew in heart her dreams would become reality.

eighteen

The weekend arrived, and Frank took Cadi out for dinner—without his children. The kids would have kicked up more of a fuss if Frank hadn't promised they'd attend Riverview with Cadi the next morning. After services and children's church, they drove to his folks' condo for lunch, Cadi and her aunt Lou in tow. The fact that Cadi was undaunted about meeting his folks impressed Frank, and everyone seemed to get along just fine. When they left, Mom hugged and kissed him good-bye before whispering, "It's good to see my boy happy again."

Frank gently reminded her that he was hardly a "boy," although Mom had the rest of the statement correct; he felt happy again.

In the days following, Frank found himself lost in his thoughts of Cadi more often than not. His coworkers took note of his distractedness, and one guy asked why he suddenly volunteered for every trip to the courthouse in Waterloo that arose.

"Gotta be a woman."

Frank didn't deny it, which fueled the jibes and snickers, but he tried to act less obvious—and stay out on patrol a lot more.

Good grief! He never remembered behaving so love struck in all his life!

Then, almost a week later, on a rainy August morning, Bettyanne Binder paid Frank a visit. He had just finished a night shift, and he planned to get home, catch a few winks, then gather up the kids and visit Cadi this evening. He hoped whatever the elderly woman required wouldn't take loads of his time.

Frank stood as the secretary showed her to his cubicle.

"Hi, Mrs. Binder. What can I do for you?"

She held up his business card and waved it. "I have a crime to report."

"All right." He helped her into a chair, wondering if the same teenagers he'd busted for underage drinking and disturbing the peace recently were wreaking more havoc in town.

"What happened?"

She removed her plastic rain bonnet and shook it out before smoothing down the skirt of her pale-blue-and-white-checked dress. "I was robbed—that's what happened. Just look at this!"

Frank sat on the edge of his desk and watched as the older woman pulled a folded piece of paper from her ivory canvas purse. She handed it to him.

He took and examined it. "This is a copy of a canceled check."

"Exactly. Now look at the back of it. That hen scratch doesn't belong to me!"

He arched his brows. "You're telling me this isn't your signature?"

"Precisely. Why, I have lovely penmanship, always did, and it certainly doesn't resemble that—that scribble on the back of the check!"

Frank studied the copy again before glancing up at Mrs. Binder. "Maybe you should start from the beginning. How did you obtain this copy?"

"Well, when the insurance money from that dreadful explosion didn't come and didn't come, I finally called. The company told me the paperwork was initially misplaced but that they had found it and my claim finally got processed. I waited a while longer and called again. But the gal on the phone said the check was issued and that it had been cashed. Needless to say, I was astonished." The woman's vein-lined hand fluttered to the base of her slim neck. "I insisted I never received the money, and that's when they sent me the copy you have in your hand."

"Looks like the check was cashed at the First Bank of

Wind Lake." He stood and walked around his desk. "Did you speak with the manager over there?"

"No. I just picked that up at the post office this morning. I haven't had a chance to speak with anyone." Her hands trembled. "I'm just so very upset."

"I understand. Let me make a phone call or two."

Opening the drawer, he pulled out the phone book, found the number, and called the bank. Leslie Pensky, the manager, couldn't recall who'd cashed the check over a month ago. When Frank asked about the cameras positioned in the lobby, she told him they were self-rewinding devices and only caught and retained a week's worth of activity at a time.

He thanked her for the info then ended the call.

"Well. . ." He rubbed his jaw in contemplation. "This is going to take further investigation."

"Deputy, I already know who stole my money." She shifted her slight frame in the chair. "It was that girl who helped me fill out the insurance forms. The blond from Waterloo."

"Cadi?" Frank shook his head. "No way."

But a moment later, the image of her aunt's new sedan fluttered through his mind. He recalled that Cadi had purchased it for her, and when he'd first seen the sleek gray car, he remarked on the generous gift. He meant to inquire about it further because his curiosity got the better of him, but then he became distracted by the kids, along with his own emotions, and forgot all about it. The fact was, whenever he was with Cadi, all he could think about was her. What's more, he thought about her even when they weren't together.

"She's the thief, I tell you!"

"Impossible. Cadi isn't capable of committing a crime." He tamped down his suspicion and inspected the canceled copy again. "Besides, how would she have gotten ahold of your check?"

"Maybe she drove into Wind Lake and asked for it at the post office."

"Did you ask Stan about that?" The Wind Lake post office

wasn't large, and everyone knew Stan Smith, the postmaster.

"I haven't had a chance to ask him." Tears formed in the older woman's eyes. "But I often have other people collect my mail for me. Sometimes they are out-of-town friends whom Stan doesn't know. They're visiting me and want to go into town for some reason, and I ask them to pick up my mail. They give Stan my name, and he hands it over."

"Probably not a good practice."

"Apparently not." Mrs. Binder's chin quivered. "A body can't trust anyone these days. Which brings me back to the reason I'm here. Cadi could have pretended like she was doing me a favor and gotten my check at the post office. I'm sure she stole it."

Frank shook his head. "Cadi wouldn't steal your check."

"Well, I want to press charges!" She balled a fist and did her best to slam it into the palm of her other hand. "I heard from a reputable source that this kind of thing happened in this town once before."

Frank winced, knowing full well Mrs. Binder was correct.

"I won't stand for it. And if you won't help me, I'll take this matter to your superiors."

"Mrs. Binder, you have no proof." Frank sensed her fear and frustration and made a special effort to soften his tone. "Now look, Cadi's my—my friend. Let me talk to her and look into this matter further and I'll get back to you, okay?"

"But I've been waiting for my money."

"Pressing charges won't get you your money any sooner. But I promise to speak with Cadi right away, and I'll pursue any leads that might result from our conversation. In the meantime, you let me know if there are any new developments on your end. All right?" Frank helped her up from the chair. "Let's be in contact on Monday morning. And I strongly suggest that from now on, you don't let anyone collect your mail for you."

Mrs. Binder replied with an exasperated sigh but eventually agreed to Frank's terms and left the office.

Once she'd gone, he lowered himself into his desk chair

and contemplated the situation. He was tired from working all night, and he hated how his fatigued mind conjured up all kinds of questions and doubts about Cadi. He could rationalize almost everything except that new car she had purchased for her aunt. That suspicion was hard to shake.

Then Mrs. Binder's words echoed in his thoughts. *"I heard from a reputable source that this kind of thing happened in this town once before."* Frank remembered, all too well, the cheating, the looting, and the devastated citizens who were left with nothing after the bogus charity group left town. He refused to believe Cadi was in the same category as those now-convicted thieves. She was the most honest, genuine woman he'd ever known.

But had he been duped? The thought sent a chill through him.

Dear God, not again!

&

Cadi finished her phone calls to Meg, Jeff, Bailey, and Will; Disaster Busters had been summoned across the state again. This time to Fort Dodge where heavy rains caused rivers to rise and neighborhoods to flood. Rescue efforts were under way.

Cadi thought of the upcoming weekend and her plans with Frank. She hated to leave town. She'd been so looking forward to seeing him and his kids again. That, combined with the fact this emergency was flood related, tempted her to refuse the request for Disaster Busters' assistance. The memory of what happened to her family in a flash flood caused a renewed sense of panic to surge through her.

But, no. She couldn't give in to fear and back out. People needed her help. She had to go—and time was of the essence.

She punched in Frank's office number. When she reached his voice mail at work, she tried his cell phone. Another recording picked up, and this time she left a message. She explained the details of Disaster Busters' latest recruitment and cited its location. She knew she was babbling, but she hoped it kept the mounting trepidation out of her tone.

At last she disconnected the call and glanced at her watch. She'd have just enough time to go home and pack up her things before she met the team back here at church.

Locking up the office, she walked through the empty halls and out into the parking lot. The rain had slowed to a drizzle. She reached her van and felt both pleased and surprised when she spotted a squad car pulling into the lot. She knew it was Frank. With a smile she waved and watched as he pulled alongside her vehicle.

He opened the door and got out. Cadi walked around the front of her minivan to meet him.

"Got a minute?"

"Sure." She noted his somewhat gruff demeanor. "Anything wrong?"

"Can we talk inside?"

"Sure, but I don't have a lot of time." Cadi led him back into Riverview's large facility. "Did you get my phone message?"

"No, I haven't had a chance to check messages."

Judging by his tone, Cadi knew she hadn't imagined his brusqueness. "Bad day?"

"Sort of." He released a weary-sounding sigh. "I'm exhausted."

"I can tell." She unlocked her office door and let him inside. "Want some coffee? It's a couple of hours old, but it's in a thermal pot."

"No, thanks. Cadi, look, I'm here on business, and I'm afraid it's not pleasant."

"What's going on?"

He pulled a piece of white paper out of his back pocket, unfolded it, and handed it to her. "Take a look at that."

Cadi took the proffered document and noticed the obvious. She held a copy of a canceled check made out to Bettyanne Binder for a large sum of money. She remembered helping the elderly woman fill out the insurance claim form.

"Mrs. Binder must be pleased."

"She would be—if she had been the one to cash the check."

"What?" Cadi felt a puzzled frown dip her brows.

"See the signature on the back of the check? Mrs. Binder insists it's not hers."

Cadi looked at the back side of the copy before glancing up at Frank again. "I don't understand."

He sat down on the corner of her desk, one leg dangling over the side. "Mrs. Binder believes someone managed to steal her check, forge a semblance of her signature, and get the cash." He paused, and Cadi saw his gaze flick over her. "She's sure that 'someone' is you, and she wants to press charges."

"What? But that's ridiculous."

"I know."

Cadi didn't think he sounded convinced, and a sickening dread fell over her. "You think I stole it, too?" The words came forth with significant effort.

"I don't think you stole it, but—"

"But?" She shook her head, remembering how he'd falsely accused her when they first met. It pained her to think he still didn't trust her.

"Cadi, look—"

"Oh, don't waste your breath. I can see the guilty verdict written all over your face."

"Bear with me, okay?" A muscle worked in his jaw, and Cadi wondered if he was about to lose his patience. "Since Mrs. Binder named you, specifically, I wanted to bring this to you myself. I didn't want one of the other officers to come to you with her complaint."

"Well, I don't know who cashed this thing." She gave back the copy of the check. "It certainly wasn't me."

Frank folded the paper and stuffed it into his pocket again. "So, you never did tell me—how were you able to purchase your aunt's new car?"

"How was I. . . ?" She blinked. "You never asked until now. What a coincidence." She stepped closer to him. "You think I stole that lady's money, don't you?"

"No, I'm not accusing you of anything. I'm inquiring."

Cadi shook her head to the contrary. "You're investigating. There's a major difference." She placed her hands on her hips and narrowed her gaze. How could she love a man who seemed so ready to convict her of a crime?

"Investigating is my job. Just for the sake of discussion, would you mind answering my question?"

"Yeah, I do mind—but I'll answer it because I have nothing to hide."

A stony expression, but one that seemed mixed with regret, settled over his features.

"I received a settlement from my car accident. You're brilliant enough to figure out the rest."

"Can you prove it?"

"Do I have to?"

He appeared to weigh his reply, but before he could actually answer, Cadi backed down. She didn't have time for this. She made her way to the file cabinet and opened the drawer in which she kept personal documents because she had nowhere to lock them up in her bedroom at home. She pulled out a folder containing the legal documents in question. Then she strode back to Frank, and it was all she could do to keep from flinging it at him.

He leafed through the file then handed it back.

"Satisfied?"

"Yeah. Thanks."

He stood to leave, and as he opened the door, Cadi's heart twisted. How could he accuse her and walk away? Just like that?

"Frank. . ."

He paused, glanced over his shoulder, then turned his body toward her.

"I can't fathom how you could even imagine that I'd steal something like another person's insurance check and forge their signature. It was one thing to be suspicious of me before we knew each other, but you and I. . ." She couldn't finish for fear she'd choke on the rest of her sentence.

His features softened. "Cadi, I *had* to ask—"

"But you should have *known*."

He shook his head. "I was acting on Mrs. Binder's accusations."

"Which are nonsense." Cadi fought back her tears. "You believed her, not me. You suspected the worst of me. How could you?"

"How?" He took a step forward. "Because I'm good at my job. I know *anyone* at *anytime* is capable of *anything*, given the right circumstances. If you don't believe me, read the Bible. King David comes to mind. He was an anointed man of God, yet he committed adultery and murder."

"That much is true, but you missed the point. I'm talking about a fundamental premise here. Trust. All good relationships are based on trust. Even the foundation of our faith is based on trust; we trust Jesus Christ and His work on the cross for our eternal salvation. We trust God with our present. Our future." She raised her arms, palms up, in an emphatic shrug. "If you don't trust me, what kind of relationship can we ever hope to have? Nothing. We have nothing."

"Nothing, huh?" His expression hardened. "I'm sorry you feel that way."

He wheeled around and left the office, pulling the door closed with a finality that shattered Cadi's heart.

nineteen

Frank fumed all the way back to Wind Lake.

Nothing. She said we have nothing. I suppose she thinks the last couple of months have been a waste of time, too.

Frank refused to admit Cadi's reaction might have been legitimate. He'd *had* to ask her about the insurance check. He'd merely been doing his job.

Hadn't he?

He shook off any doubts. He was in the right to question her, especially after Mrs. Binder went so far as to name Cadi as the one who stole her insurance check.

Except, in his heart, he'd known Cadi was innocent all along.

His grip tightened on the steering wheel of the squad car. Perhaps he should have told her from the start that he'd defended her to Mrs. Binder. Maybe it would have prevented those angry sparks he'd seen in her blue eyes. Sure, he had questions. But she'd answered them—right before she said they had "nothing."

Does she really feel that way?

Frank stopped at the office, dropped off the squad car, then drove home in his own vehicle. Knowing his kids were with Lois today, he walked into the adjacent townhouse to say hello. The noise level in the finished basement rec room was off the charts because rain had forced Lois to move the daycare center indoors. But Dustin and Emmie were having fun, and since Lois didn't mind, he decided he'd leave them there so he could get a few hours of sleep. His limbs felt weighted from exhaustion.

"Don't worry, Dad, we'll be sure to wake you up when it's time to go to Cadi's house."

Frank refrained from growling at his son. Hadn't this been exactly what he'd feared? Cadi's calling it quits and his kids getting hurt?

He made his way next door. His brain felt muddled from lack of sleep.

Did she really say to call it quits?

Fatigue clouded his ability to reason, although one thing he knew for sure: His life would never be the same without Cadi.

❧

"The Des Moines River continues to rise. Experts say it will crest four feet above flood stage. Many roads have already become impassable, so motorists are advised to take precautions."

Cadi turned up the radio in the minivan.

"In low-lying areas, floodwaters have submerged street signs and carried away everything from ice machines to netted soccer goals. It's reported that as many as twenty thousand people are without power."

"Great," she muttered. "Just great."

"We're going to live up to our name this weekend," Will quipped from where he sat in the passenger seat. "Disaster Busters."

"Do you want me to drive, Cadi?" Jeff called to her from the backseat.

"No, I'm okay."

"Well, at this speed, we'll never get there. I don't think I've ever seen you drive so slow."

She wrestled with the idea of giving up control of her vehicle, but in the end she knew Jeff was right. In this instance, her anxiety made her overly cautious, and she sensed her team's growing impatience.

Pulling over onto the shoulder, Cadi allowed her friend to take the wheel. She crawled into the bucket seat across from Bailey, secured her seat belt and shoulder strap, then forced her taut nerves to relax. Will tuned the radio in to a Christian station, and Cadi forced herself not to think about what lie ahead or dwell on the heated verbal exchange she'd had with Frank. But it was no use. She couldn't shake either subject from her thoughts.

"You're so quiet, Cadi," Meg said. "Aren't you feeling well?"

"I'm fine. I—I just have a lot on my mind right now."

"Did Frank pop the question?"

"Oh, he 'popped' several, but none was the question you're referring to—that's for sure." Cadi turned in her seat and regarded her best friend. She noted the teasing gleam in Meg's hazel eyes, but Cadi wasn't up to the goading. Or the banter. "Seriously, I'd rather not talk about it."

Meg searched her face then nodded. "Okay."

With the subject of Frank now dropped, Cadi tried again to push aside her tumultuous emotions. She focused on prayer in preparation for the flooding situation that she and the rest of the team would soon encounter.

An hour later, Jeff pulled the van into the parking lot of the New Elk Lodge, a huge facility and part of a campground. It had opened its doors to rescue personnel and those seeking immediate shelter. After checking in, they were directed farther down the highway. They walked the rest of the way beneath a gloomy sky.

"At least the rain stopped," Meg said, sounding cheery.

"For now," Will added. "More is on the way."

Cadi suppressed a groan.

When they arrived on the scene, they were met with controlled chaos. Many residents had been able to evacuate while some refused to leave their homes. Others, however, were trapped.

After speaking with the fire chief, one of the men heading up the rescue efforts, Will approached Cadi and the rest of the Disaster Busters team. "Okay, here's the scoop. We're going to help get folks out of their houses. We'll cover this cul-de-sac." He gave a nod, indicating to the area just over his shoulder. "It's about a quarter of a mile long, and as you all can see, it goes downhill and curves to the left. We're standing on the high end." He looked at Cadi. "Since the water is overflow from the river and not due to a flash flood, most rescuers are wading in. Every boat, other than those privately owned, is being used to evacuate elderly and handicapped residents."

"We can walk. Let's go," Jeff said eagerly.

"One last thing." A serious expression spread across Will's face. "We've only got a few hours until dark, and more rain is on the way. The water level on the street is expected to rise."

Cadi looked down the flooded, tree-lined neighborhood and squelched her fears before they could resurface. *I can do this, Lord. With Your help, I can do anything.*

"Are you going to be all right, Cadi?"

She turned and found Bailey regarding her with a concerned expression. "I'll be fine," she said with more confidence than she felt. "This is nothing like the horrible rushing water that my family and I were caught in when I was a kid." She glanced at the gray sky. "I just hope the rain holds off."

"We've got to be done by the time it's dark," Will repeated. "There's no power in this area. We'll need to take flashlights."

Jeff clapped his hands then rubbed his palms together. "Let's get our gear and go."

After pulling on protective waders and collecting their flashlights, the Disaster Busters team made its way into the deluge. Cadi's pulse raced with each step she took, but she kept reminding herself that people needed her help and that an almighty God walked right along with her.

ঌ

After four hours of sleep and two cups of strong coffee, Frank felt like a new man. While the kids ate supper at their grandparents' next door, he opened his Bible and read several chapters. He was amazed at the way his skewed world righted itself once he allowed God's Word to steer his thought processes.

He phoned Cadi, intending to begin with an apology, but only reached her voice mail. Either she was really angry, Frank reasoned, or she couldn't hear her cell phone. Knowing Cadi, he figured it was more the latter since she was forgiving to a fault. But would she agree to continue their relationship, or had he finally crossed the line with the way he'd handled the Binder insurance check situation?

Lord, I hope I didn't do permanent damage here.

He mulled things over and remembered Cadi saying this morning that she'd left a message for him. Locating his cell phone, Frank accessed his messages. He listened to her lengthy recording in which she canceled their plans this weekend because of the flood situation across the state. He heard the apprehension in her voice, and his chest constricted at the thought that he'd let her down. Instead of encouragement, he had most likely added to her stress. He wondered what he could do to make it up to her.

He paced the living room floor and shot up an arrow of a prayer for wisdom. Flowers and candy wouldn't do the trick, because Cadi was out of town. She couldn't be reached by phone.

I'll just have to find her and tell her in person.

Tell her what?

Frank stopped and placed his hands on his hips. He figured he'd start off by apologizing for his boorish behavior this morning. He'd let Cadi know he was wrong for questioning her integrity and that he—well, he just couldn't imagine his life without her.

His home phone jangled, and he answered it at once, hoping it might be Cadi. Instead, it was another sheriff's deputy.

"Hey, listen, I know you're off duty," the officer began, "but I've got this lady here—Mrs. Binder."

"She's there? At the office?" Frank felt a heavy frown settle on his brows. "What's going on?"

"She says it's urgent that she speak with you. She says you know the situation."

"Yeah, okay. Put her on." Frank drew in a deep breath and lowered himself onto the couch. Moments later, he heard

Mrs. Binder's gentle but determined voice.

"Deputy Parker, I won't need to press charges. I have my money."

Surprised by the turn of events, Frank sat forward and prompted her to continue.

"Well, you see, on the day my check arrived, I had a hair appointment. The post office closed at noon, seeing it was a Saturday, so my, um, gentleman friend," she said, sounding suddenly bashful, "offered to pick up my mail. When he saw that my check had come, he walked over to the beauty parlor and had me sign it. Then he dashed to the bank to cash it because the bank also closes earlier on Saturday. Well, I suppose you know that. Anyway, he gave me the money, but I scarcely recall him doing so because I was engrossed in a very important conversation with Lorna Flores. She heads up the committee for our quilting club."

Frank couldn't help a small grin.

"Needless to say, that explains my chicken scratch of a signature. I wasn't paying attention to what I was doing. Later on, after I arrived home, I changed purses, although I never did see the envelope with the money that I had zipped into the side pocket for safekeeping."

He cringed, imagining the scenario. "Just a word of warning for the future, Mrs. Binder: You should never carry such a large sum in your purse or keep it in your home."

"Yes, I know. You're absolutely right. The bank is the safest place. But, you see, my account isn't with the bank in Wind Lake. My gentleman friend does his financial business there and the girls all know him. They call him Grampa Grapes." She laughed. "His last name is Grapenwald."

Frank recognized the name immediately. "Are you referring to Harold Grapenwald? He worked as a janitor and general handyman at the high school until he retired. He's known around town as a guy who'll help anybody and who can fix almost anything."

"That's Harold." Mrs. Binder sounded both pleased and

proud. "Anyway," she said, her voice growing solemn once more, "the long and short of it is, he thought he was doing me a favor even though I could have just as easily taken the check to my own bank that following Monday."

"I see." Frank saw no reason not to believe her, as careless and ridiculous as it might seem to him. After all, he'd heard stranger explanations in his line of work. He'd learned truth was definitely weirder than fiction.

"I told Harold about my visit to your office today." A short pause. "He's been on a fishing trip in Canada and just got back. I haven't talked to him in weeks—until this afternoon. When I mentioned pressing charges against Cadi, he reminded me that he'd cashed the check for me."

"You understand, Mrs. Binder, that's it's a serious thing to accuse someone of theft and forgery." Frank felt as if he were reprimanding himself as well as the older woman.

"I realize that, although it's not like I dragged Cadi's name through the mud. I've only discussed this matter with two close friends, one being Harold. They're both aware the incident is no fault of Cadi's."

Frank felt appeased.

"I'm terribly sorry for any trouble I caused," she continued. "Chalk it up to an old man's good intentions and an old woman's less-than-perfect memory."

"We all forget things, even important things. Doesn't matter what age we are." He felt immensely relieved that the money had been found, but now he was doubly determined to speak with Cadi as soon as possible.

"Thank you for your understanding," Mrs. Binder said. "I'm very embarrassed, and I'll have you know I deposited the money into my bank account this afternoon."

"Good. Thanks for calling. I'm glad everything worked out."

The phone conversation ended, and Frank sat back on the sofa, forming a plan. He fired off another quick prayer that Lois would agree to babysit for the weekend. His parents could probably help out, as well.

He raked his hand through his short-cropped hair. His mind was made up. He stood and walked next door, letting himself into the house. The kids came running to greet him.

"Are we going to Cadi's now?"

Frank saw the excitement in his son's eyes and hated to disappoint him. "Cadi's not home this weekend. She got called out of town on business."

A frown of disappointment furrowed the boy's sun-streaked brows. "But she bought a new video game for me."

"There'll be time in the days ahead to play it, I'm sure." Frank saw that Lois had entered the room. He looked her way. "Cadi is assisting with the rescue operations near Fort Dodge. Major flooding over in that area. I'd like to go find her and maybe lend a hand."

"Can we come, too, Daddy?"

"No, Em." He swung the little girl up into his arms. "It's too dangerous. But I'd like to go. . . ." He looked at Lois again.

"If you're asking in a roundabout way if I'll watch my grandchildren this weekend, you know I will." She stared at him with tightlipped acquiescence. "I know how important this woman is to you."

"Yes, she's important to me."

Lois shifted her stance and slipped her slender hands into the pockets of her denim slacks. "I guess she's a nice enough person."

Frank smiled, feeling both shocked and elated by the positive remark. "How did you come to realize that?"

"She won *you* over, didn't she?"

"Sure did." He smiled.

"The biggest thing I noticed," Lois said, "is that she's succeeded where we, your family, and friends have failed. God used her to draw you back to church and back into His Word. For that reason alone, I've decided Cadi's a special person."

"She is. She's very special." Frank felt like his mother-in-law's comments were affirmation for tonight's plans. He knew he was doing the right thing, even if it meant driving hours in the rain in order to talk to Cadi.

He looked at Dustin and Emily. "You two behave for your grandma. I've got my phone, and you can call me." He hesitated for a moment. "Maybe you can talk to Cadi, too, if she's not busy."

And if she's still speaking to me, he added silently.

twenty

Cadi glanced up just as large droplets of rain fell from the darkening sky. By now the floodwater was hip-high in some areas on the street, and every muscle in her body ached. Her legs felt waterlogged. For a good part of the afternoon, she and her team helped people pack some of their belongings and cajoled others who insisted on staying. So far as Cadi knew, everyone on the cul-de-sac had evacuated.

All except the Manskis, who'd changed their minds at the last minute. They'd been bent on staying until their neighbors convinced them otherwise. And now, as Cadi carried boxes out of their house and loaded them into an aluminum rowboat that Mr. Manski had stored in his garage, she prayed they'd finish before the last of their daylight vanished.

"Okay, is that it?" She heaved a box over the side of the small, floating craft.

"Well, let me think. . . ."

Cadi suppressed a groan as the middle-aged woman began to ponder for the umpteenth time. She sat in the boat while her husband stood in the water at the helm, ready to pull his wife and property to higher ground. Unfortunately, his better half was having trouble making up her mind about what to take and what to leave behind. Cadi felt trapped between Mr. Manski's impatience and his wife's indecision.

"Mrs. Manski, there's really no time left." Cadi knew that, at the request of the fire chief, the Disaster Busters crew, along with the last of the emergency personnel, had vacated the cul-de-sac almost forty-five minutes ago. None of the Disaster Busters team knew she had stayed behind to help, and she could only imagine how frantic Meg, Will, Jeff, and Bailey would be as they searched for her. It didn't, however, match her own escalating fear of being in floodwater after dark.

"Look," she told the Manskis, "this is our opportunity to get out of here safely. We need to go."

A bolt of anxiety shot through Cadi when she thought again of the late hour, the rain, and the murky river water. Even so, she felt sure she'd manage if she held on to the boat and the Manskis were with her.

"Maybe I should take—oh, wait—I guess those items can stay, too."

"We're leaving Anita," her husband said. "No more stuff."

"I agree." Cadi peered down the long street, but because of the bend in the road and the encroaching darkness, she couldn't see the other rescue personnel.

"Wait." Anita Manski began to push to her feet.

"Don't stand up!" Cadi's heart did a flip as she imagined the petite woman falling overboard and cracking her head on some unseen object.

"Honey, I moved a lot of stuff upstairs." The man pulled off his baseball cap and rubbed his balding head. "You can make a list of what you want and I'll get it tomorrow."

Cadi wanted to encourage that call to action. "Good plan, Mr. Manski." She grabbed hold of the stern. "I'll push, you pull."

"Oh, my purse. I've got to have my purse." Anita Manski swung her gaze from Cadi to her husband. "My medication and my wallet are in there along with my cell phone and address book."

Sam Manski fired off a string of obscenities that burned Cadi's ears. "If you think I'm going to fetch it," he added, "you're out of your mind."

"Well, maybe we should have just stayed put."

"Too late for that now!"

"Please, stop bickering. I'll go back into the house and get the purse." Cadi realized it might be foolish to waste already borrowed time, but if Mrs. Manski required her medication, *someone* had to retrieve it.

"You'll need the keys," the older woman said. "Sam, give her the house keys."

He trudged around and placed his thick key ring in Cadi's palm. "Make it snappy, okay?"

"You got it."

"My purse is on the dining room buffet. It's a fawn-colored, leather handbag."

"It's a suitcase," her husband groused.

Maybe we should have used it as a floatation device. Cadi tried not to huff about it as she waded through the water and climbed the wooden porch steps. Inside the Cape Cod home, she strained to see in the unlit rooms. Only too late did she realize she'd left her flashlight in the boat with the Manskis. She hadn't been able to carry the large flashlight and boxes, too, so she'd set down the battery-powered light and then forgotten it. Unfortunately for her, there wasn't time to go back out to the boat and retrieve it. She'd have to fumble her way through the place and find Mrs. Manski's purse.

She gazed around. Everything was unfamiliar, yet she recalled glimpsing the dining room to the left of the front door.

She felt her way to what she believed was the buffet and knocked into an object that clanged against the floor. She winced, hesitated, then moved on.

Hurry. I have to hurry.

She continued to feel her way through the room.

No purse.

She touched her way to the other side and tried again, but this time she tripped over something and fell. Unhurt, she pushed to her feet. Seconds later, she recognized the object over which she'd just stumbled: the leather handbag!

Relief engulfed her as Cadi lifted the heavy purse, slinging its strap over her shoulder. She picked her way back through the house. When she reached the porch, the dense downpour combined with the water lapping against the steps gave her great pause. She tried to see beyond the sheets of rain but couldn't make out a single thing, and she wasn't about to wade into the blackness of the floodwater on her own.

"Mr. and Mrs. Manski? I found the purse!"

She listened for a reply.

Nothing but the din of the falling rain.

She called again, but no one answered.

Once more. But no response.

In the next moment, Cadi came head-to-head with her worst nightmare: She was stranded, alone, with darkness surrounding her, and the river rising.

❧

"Cadi's missing!"

"What?" Frank exited the SUV and pulled the hood of his rain gear over his head. He stared at Meg. He could see she'd been out in the elements for some time and her plastic poncho was of little use anymore. "What do you mean she's missing?"

"We were helping with the evacuation," she said, throwing a thumb over her shoulder. "We were supposed to quit when it got dark, and we agreed to meet at the checkpoint, but Cadi hasn't shown up. Jeff was the last one to see her. He said she was at the end of the block, on the cul-de-sac, helping people gather up their stuff. He thought she was right behind him, but apparently she wasn't. Next we located the folks she'd been assisting, the Manskis. They said they assumed she'd followed them to higher ground." Meg's voice strained from unshed emotion. "Obviously she didn't, and now we can't find her!"

"She's not in the lodge?" Frank had been in the facility but hadn't bothered to look around. He'd been told emergency personnel were downhill a ways from the campsite.

"We've searched the lodge twice. No sign of Cadi. But I was just on my way up there again for another look when I ran into you."

"Here, take my vehicle; don't walk." He handed her the keys. "Where's everyone else?"

Meg turned and pointed to her distant left. "Jeff and Will

volunteered to hunt for Cadi, but the cops won't let them beyond the barricades. Orders from headquarters and all that."

"That seems odd. Why wouldn't they form a rescue party to locate Cadi?"

"Because it's not a mandatory evacuation situation. Some residents chose to stay in their homes, flooded or not. The cops feel Cadi's safe until morning, but. . ." Meg almost choked on her words, and Frank knew she was extremely upset. "But they don't know Cadi's history. If she's out there, even if she's safe, she's got to be terrified."

"I agree." Frank wiped the rain out of his eyes and reran the information through his mind. It pained him to think of Cadi trapped in what was obviously a frightening situation for her.

Lord, please protect her.

Frank urged Meg into the shelter of his SUV and suggested she drive to the lodge and dry out for a while.

"And don't worry," he added. "We'll find Cadi."

He walked the rest of the way down the road and spotted the three remaining Disaster Busters members. They filled him in, stating, just as Meg had, that Cadi was still somewhere out in the flooded area.

"It's my fault." Jeff had to raise his voice to be heard above the downpour. "I told her earlier this afternoon to face her fears. She was probably trying to prove something and pushed herself further than she should have."

"Well, let's not jump to conclusions." Frank noticed none of them laid any blame on him for Cadi's disappearance. He wondered if they knew about this morning's confrontation. He felt responsible for her, and he realized he'd never forgive himself if the unspeakable happened to Cadi. He had to find her.

He eyed the officers standing guard at the barricades. He wondered if he knew any of them. Often enough he crossed paths with state troopers, police, and other sheriff's deputies, both within Iowa and out of state. A unique camaraderie existed among officers of the law, and Frank felt fairly confident he could enlist their help.

He looked at Bailey. She had obviously assumed his thoughts.

"When we last saw her, Cadi was unharmed, so they said if she's stranded, we'll have to wait until morning to get her. Emergency crews say there's no imminent danger, such as ruptured gas and electrical lines. All power to the area has been shut off. Even so, they won't let anyone back into the area because of safety concerns. Sounds like an oxymoron to me."

"Well, I can see their point," Frank said, although he understood Bailey's side, too. "Someone might slip and fall and drown, and then the family could sue the city, county, and state for not protecting its citizens."

"I get it, Frank. But I can't handle the thought of Cadi cold and wet and scared to death all night. We have to do *something*."

He heartily agreed. "How deep is the water down there?"

"Not too bad," Will replied. "Maybe three feet high."

"That's bad enough," Bailey argued.

Frank rubbed his jaw, contemplating. "And you're sure Cadi's down this particular street?"

"Yep. I saw her carrying boxes from the last house on the right," Jeff said.

An idea formed. He glanced at the officers again and then back at the trio beside him.

"Listen, why don't you all head to the lodge, warm up inside, and give me some time? Say, an hour? I'll meet you up there, and maybe I'll have more answers."

❧

Cadi sat just inside the front entrance of the Manskis' home. She shivered and watched the veil of rain pour from the sky. She leaned her aching back up against the wall and, as she mulled over the events of the last ten hours, she deemed it a bad day all around.

She concluded she'd overreacted this morning with Frank. Why didn't she soothe away all his doubts instead of becoming defensive? Now she could only hope and pray he'd believe she was innocent and forgive her childish fit of temper.

Next she'd let the Manskis manipulate her, and then she'd defied the law by lingering in an area that was off-limits after nightfall. Now she faced the consequences. She hated to think how worried her friends were—and all because she didn't do what she knew was right!

Assessing her present situation once more, Cadi wondered if she could work up the courage to duck into the rain and walk up the street. Sounded easy enough. But then the gravity of the situation struck her and she envisioned the pitch-black night and the water swirling around her, and she decided there was no amount of courage on earth that would propel her through all that. She could scream for help, but no one would hear her above the rain, and she'd likely drain the last of her energy, just upsetting herself further.

She reached into her sweatshirt pocket and pulled out her cell phone. She tried to place a call again, but just as before, it was no use. No signal.

So, now what? Ride it out and wait until morning?

Cadi closed her eyes and prayed. She willed herself to relax. Breathe. Think of something positive. A picnic with Frank and his kids on a gorgeous summer day. No rain. Just sunny, cloudless skies. No angry words. Only mutual adulation.

"Cadi!"

She snapped to attention. She listened. Had she imagined it?

"Cadi!"

The voice was unmistakably Frank's, and moments later she flinched as a bright beam shone in her eyes. It moved away then returned, illuminating the open entryway of the home.

She squinted. "Frank, is that you?"

"Yep." His voice grew closer.

Disbelief and joy swept over her. She shielded her eyes

from the blinding light as he approached. "What are you doing here?"

"Courting disaster. What does it look like?"

Cadi almost laughed.

Almost.

Instead, she stood and hurried onto the porch. She met him on the stairs and threw her arms around him. She pressed her cheek against his cold, wet jaw. "I've never been so happy to see anyone in my life!"

"I was hoping you'd say that." She felt his strong arm close around her waist as he held her.

She took great comfort in the fact that he didn't seem angry. Nevertheless, she owed him an apology.

"I'm sorry about this morning. I have such a hotheaded temper. My mouth runs off without my—"

He silenced her with a kiss. "Cadi, I'm the one who should be saying I'm sorry. I never should have doubted you—you, of all people."

"You trust me? You really do?"

"Yes, Cadi, I do."

Sudden tears obscured her vision, and her pent-up emotions gave way.

"Shh, don't cry." He held her for several long moments more before moving back a few paces. "I think we'd best finish this conversation later."

She sniffed.

He pulled an orange floatation device off his forearm. "I managed to get this life jacket, and I could have waited while some officers rustled up a boat for me to use, but I figured by the time they found one, I could have fetched you and been back on higher ground." He slipped the preserver over her head and secured it.

"Ready?"

"No, wait." Cadi remembered Mrs. Manski's purse and Mr. Manski's keys. She ran into the house, grabbed the items, and returned to the porch steps.

"All set?"

"Yes."

He took her hand and led her down each step; however, she made the mistake of glancing across the ominous body of water. Panic gripped her as memories of her childhood disaster overwhelmed her common sense. She froze and looped her arm around the last rung of the rail.

"What's the matter?"

"I—I can't do this," she stammered.

"Yes, you can. I've got a secure hold on you." He gave her hand a squeeze. "And a few yards away, the water's shallower. This is the deepest part." He paused and gently tugged at her arm. "Come on. You'll be fine."

Cadi's mouth felt parched and her throat tight, making a reply impossible.

Frank stepped in beside her and placed his lips close to her ear. "There's no way I'll let anything happen to you." He placed a kiss on the side of her head. "I can't imagine my life without you, Cadi, and that's the honest truth. I don't know when it happened—maybe the first minute I saw you in Wind Lake, but I'm in love with you."

Her fears dissipated. She turned to stare at him while happiness swelled inside of her. She'd dreamed of hearing him say that he loved her, and now her dream had come true.

She let go of the railing and clung to him. "I love you, too, Frank."

She wanted to say more, much more, but he suddenly moved with lightning speed. He whisked her off the step, into the blinding rain, and through the water. Before she could react, they'd reached the shallowest section of the flooded street. Several more steps and their feet were no longer submerged, but on wet pavement. The last of her fear evaporated, although her limbs felt weak from the hours of physical labor and the chill from the water.

She stopped to catch her breath. "That was some kind of trick, but it worked. You got me off the porch."

He caught her gaze and held it. Cadi could just barely see the meaningful glint in his eyes.

"Just for the record, I meant every word."

Her joy was renewed.

"Let's get out of this rain. Think you can make it up the hill?" Frank shined the flashlight toward the wet asphalt highway.

She smiled and nodded. "With you at my side and God in my heart, I think I can make it anywhere."

She clutched Frank's hand, her fingers entwined with his, and she held on tight as they made their way to the lodge.

epilogue

Eight months later

Fresh, springtime floral arrangements stood in cut-glass vases near the altar, and pleated white paper wedding bells hung from Riverview Bible Church's vaulted ceiling. The pews filled with enthusiastic friends and relatives who had come to share this special day, uniting for life Frank Allen Parker and Cadence Renee Trent.

In one of the back dressing rooms, Cadi smoothed the skirt of the white satin and lace gown, a creation her great-aunt had taken pleasure in sewing.

"You look absolutely stunning," Aunt Lou said, tears brimming in her eyes.

Cadi hugged her great-aunt long and hard. "Thank you—thank you for everything."

"I'm as proud as any mother of the bride."

Pulling back, Cadi dabbed her own eyes. "Let's not start crying now. We'll look all puffy for the pictures."

"You're right." Aunt Lou sniffed and swatted an errant tear.

The prelude began, the music wafting through the church's elaborate sound system. Lois Chayton, Dustin and Emmie's grandmother, appeared at the door.

"Everyone's ready." Her eyes twinkled with happiness.

Over the months, Cadi had gotten better acquainted with Lois. Despite her gruffness, Cadi discovered that Lois had a caring nature and a genuine love for the Lord. Children adored her, so Lois's in-home day care was both a fitting and successful business venture. What's more, Cadi felt pleased she'd included Lois in the wedding party. She made a fantastic wedding director, and she wasn't shy about ordering people into their places.

"You're on," Lois said.

Cadi took Aunt Lou's arm, and they strolled through the hallway and into the expansive lobby. Bailey and Jeff, the last of the bridal party to walk down the aisle, were already halfway to the altar.

The wedding march began to play, and Cadi couldn't believe the moment she had dreamed of for so long was finally at hand. Her groom awaited her, looking dapper in his dark tux. Dustin and Emmie stood beside him, looking like miniature versions of the bride and groom.

An usher laid out the white bridal runner, and then Aunt Lou escorted Cadi to the front of the sanctuary. Cadi hardly noticed their friends and family crowded into the many rows of padded seats as her gaze affixed to Frank's. He seemed to fill every one of her senses.

They reached the altar, and after her aunt "gave her away," Cadi slipped her hand around Frank's elbow. Both Pastor Dremond and Pastor Connor took a turn challenging Frank and Cadi in their new life together. Next they recited their vows, and finally the pastors pronounced them united in matrimony.

Pastor Dremond gave Frank a wry smile. "You may kiss your bride."

Frank turned and cupped Cadi's face with his hands. "My beautiful, sassy bride," he whispered with a mix of adoration and amusement shining in his dark eyes.

"My handsome hero."

They kissed, and Cadi decided her weak knees and heart's song were more than part of a fairy-tale finale to a perfect wedding ceremony. Rather, they signified her entire happily-ever-after as Mrs. Frank Parker.

A Letter To Our Readers

Dear Reader:

In order that we might better contribute to your reading enjoyment, we would appreciate your taking a few minutes to respond to the following questions. We welcome your comments and read each form and letter we receive. When completed, please return to the following:

Fiction Editor
Heartsong Presents
PO Box 719
Uhrichsville, Ohio 44683

1. Did you enjoy reading *Courting Disaster* by Andrea Boeshaar?
   ❑ Very much! I would like to see more books by this author!
   ❑ Moderately. I would have enjoyed it more if

   _____

   _____

   _____

2. Are you a member of **Heartsong Presents**? ❑ Yes ❑ No
   If no, where did you purchase this book? _____

   _____

3. How would you rate, on a scale from 1 (poor) to 5 (superior), the cover design? _____

4. On a scale from 1 (poor) to 10 (superior), please rate the following elements.

   _____ Heroine   _____ Plot
   _____ Hero   _____ Inspirational theme
   _____ Setting   _____ Secondary characters

5. These characters were special because? _____

_____

_____

6. How has this book inspired your life? _____

_____

_____

7. What settings would you like to see covered in future
   Heartsong Presents books? _____

_____

_____

8. What are some inspirational themes you would like to see
   treated in future books? _____

_____

_____

9. Would you be interested in reading other **Heartsong
   Presents** titles? ❏ Yes ❏ No

10. Please check your age range:
     ❏ Under 18   ❏ 18-24
     ❏ 25-34   ❏ 35-45
     ❏ 46-55   ❏ Over 55

Name _____
Occupation _____
Address _____
City, State, Zip _____

OHIO
Weddings

3 stories in 1

Step onto Bay Island and be touched by love. In a small Ohio community on Lake Erie, three remarkable women reexamine their lives. Will these three women ever be the same after the waves of change set their hearts adrift?

Contemporary, paperback, 368 pages, 5³⁄₁₆" x 8"

Presents

Great Inspirational Romance at a Great Price!

Heartsong Presents books are inspirational romances in contemporary and historical settings, designed to give you an enjoyable, spirit-lifting reading experience. You can choose wonderfully written titles from some of today's best authors like Wanda E. Brunstetter, Mary ConneC, Susan Page Davis, Cathy Marie Hake, Joyce Livingston, and many others.

When ordering quantities less than twelve, above titles are $2.97 each.
Not all titles may be available at time of order.